THE
MARYLEBONE
DROP

Books by Mick Herron

The Oxford Series
Down Cemetery Road
The Last Voice You Hear
Why We Die
Smoke & Whispers

The Slough House Series
Slow Horses
Dead Lions
The List (a novella)
Real Tigers
Spook Street
London Rules
Joe Country

Other Novels
Reconstruction
Nobody Walks
This Is What Happened
The Marylebone Drop (a novella)

THE
MARYLEBONE
DROP

Mick Herron

Published by
Soho Press, Inc.
853 Broadway
New York, NY 10003

Library of Congress Cataloging-in-Publication Data

Herron, Mick, author.
The Marylebone drop / Mick Herron.

ISBN 978-1-64129-013-5
eISBN 978-1-64129-014-2

I. Title

PR6108.E77 M37 2018 823'.92—dc23 2018027719

Printed in the United States of America

10 9 8 7 6 5 4 3 2

THE
MARYLEBONE
DROP

Seasoned Park watchers later said that the affair really began in Fischer's, that beloved "café and konditorei" that bestows a touch of early twentieth-century Vienna on the foothills of twenty-first-century Marylebone High Street; its warm interior, its spring yellows and glazed browns, a welcome refuge from the winter-drizzled pavements. The more callow of their brethren preferred to believe that it started, as all things must, at Regent's Park, but then the new generation had been trained to think itself at the constant heart of events, while the older knew that Spook Street, like Watling Street, runs backwards and forwards in time. The meeting at the Park might well have occurred earlier than the drop on Marylebone High, but that was a detail only, and when the time came for the whole business to be black-ribboned and consigned to the archive, nobody would care that a strip-lit office with functional furniture had been where the starting pistol was fired. No, once the facts were safely recorded, they'd print the legend instead. And legends thrive on local colour.

So Fischer's was the starting point; as good a place as any, and better than most. To quote from its website, "The menu includes an extensive choice of cured fish, salads, schnitzels, sausages, *brötchen* and sandwiches, *strudels*, biscuits, ice cream coupes, hot chocolates and coffees with traditional *tortes mit schlag*." How could that not set the heart racing, with its enticing umlauts, its brazen italics, its artfully roman "coupes"? Solomon Dortmund can never pick up its menu without feeling that life—even one as long as his—holds some consolations; can never put it down again without inner turmoil having raged.

Today, he has settled upon a hot chocolate—he breakfasted late, so has no need for anything substantial, but various errands having placed him in the neighbourhood, it would be unthinkable to pass Fischer's without dropping in. And his appearance is instantly celebrated: he is greeted by name by a friendly young waiter, he is guided to a table, he is assured that his chocolate has so nearly arrived that he might as well be dabbing a napkin to his lips already. To all of which Solomon, being one of those heroes whom life's cruelties have rendered gentle, responds with a kind smile. Secure at his table, he surveys the congregation: sparse today, but other people, however few in number, always command Solomon's interest, for Solomon is a people-watcher, always has been, always will be. His life having included many people who disappeared too soon, he is attentive to those who remain within sight, which today embraced an elderly pair sitting beneath the clock, and whose conversation, he feels, will mirror that device's progress, being equally regular, equally familiar, equally unlikely to surprise; three intense young men, heavily bearded, discussing politics (he hopes), or at least literature, or chess; and a pair of women in their forties who are absorbed in something one of them has summoned up on her telephone. Solomon nods benevolently. His own telephone is black, with a rotary dial, and lives on a table, but he is one of those rare creatures who recognises that even those technological developments in which he himself has neither interest nor investment might yet be of value to others, and he is perfectly content to allow them to indulge themselves. Such contemplation happily consumes the time needed to prepare his chocolate, for here comes the waiter already, and soon all is neatly arranged in front of him: cup, saucer, spoon, napkin; the elements of ritual as important as the beverage itself. Solomon Dortmund, eyes closed, takes a sip, and for one tiny moment is transported to his childhood. Few who knew him then would recognise him now. That robust child, the roly-poly infant, is now stooped and out of synch with the world. In his black coat and antique homburg, whiskers sprouting from every visible orifice, he resembles an academic whose subject has been rendered otiose. A figure of fun to those who don't know him, and he is aware of that, and regards it as one of life's better jokes. He takes another sip. This is not heaven; this is not perfection. But it is a small moment of pleasure in a world more commonly disposed to pain, and is to be treasured.

Sated for the moment, he resumes his inspection of the room. To his left, by the window, is a young blonde woman,

and Solomon allows his gaze to linger on her, for this young
woman is very attractive, in today's idiom; *beautiful* in Solomon's own, for Solomon is too old to pay heed to the ebb and
flow of linguistic fashion, and he knows beauty when he sees
it. The young woman is sorting through correspondence, which
gives Solomon a little flush of pleasure, for who today, young
or old, sorts through correspondence? Ninety per cent of what
drops through his own letterbox is junk; the other ten per cent
mere notifications of one sort or another: meter readings,
interest rates; nothing requiring a response. But this young lady
has a number of envelopes in front of her; brown envelopes of
the size codified as C5 (Solomon Dortmund knows his sta-
tionery). Job applications? He dabs his lips with his napkin.
He enjoys these little excursions into the lives of others, the
raising of unanswerable questions. He has solved, or reconciled
himself to, all the puzzles his own life is likely to throw at him.
Other peoples' remain a source of fascination. Glimpses of their
occupations are overheard prayers; doors left ajar on mysterious
existences.

He returns to his chocolate, slowing down his intake,
because endings should never be hurried. Once more, he surveys the room. The young woman has gathered her things
together; is standing, preparing to leave. A man enters, his
attention on his mobile phone. Through the momentarily open
door intrude the mid-morning sounds of Marylebone High:
a passing taxi, a skirl of laughter, the rumble of London. And
Solomon can see what is about to happen as surely as if he
were reading the scene on a page; the brief moment of impact,

the startled *oomph* from the young lady, an equally surprised *ungh* from the man, a scattering of envelopes, the sudden monopoly of attention. It takes less time to happen than it does to recount. And then the man, fully recovered, is apologising; the young woman assuring him that the fault is as much hers as his (this is not true); the envelopes are gathered up while the young lady pats at herself, confirming that she still has everything she ought to have; the bag slung over her shoulder, the scarf around her neck. It is done. The stack of envelopes is returned to her with a smile, a nod; there would have been a doffing of a hat, had the props department supplied a hat. A moment later, the man is at a table, busying himself with the buttons on his coat; the young woman is at the door, is through it, is gone. Marylebone High Street has swallowed her up. The morning continues in its unhurried way.

And Solomon Dortmund finishes his chocolate, and at length rises and settles his bill, a scrupulous ten per cent added in coins. To anyone watching as he heads for the outside world, he is no more than old-fashioned clothing on a sticklike frame; a judgement he would accept without demur. But under the hat, under the coat, under the wealth of whiskers, Solomon carries the memory of tradecraft in his bones, and those bones are rattled now by more than the winter wind.

"John," he says to himself as he steps onto the pavement. "I must speak to John."

And then he too dissolves into London's mass.

• • •

Meanwhile—or some time earlier, by the pedant's clock; the previous week, or the one before that—there was a meeting in Regent's Park. A strip-lit office, as mentioned, with functional furniture and carpet tiles, each replaceable square foot a forgettable colour and texture. The table commanding most of the floorspace had two saucer-sized holes carved into it, through which cables could be threaded when hardware needed plugging in, and along one wall was a whiteboard which, to Diana Taverner's certain knowledge, had never been used, but which nevertheless mutely declared itself the room's focal point. The chairs were H&S-approved, but only to the extent that each could hold an adult's weight; long-term occupation of any would result in backache. So far, so good, she thought. The head of the Limitations Committee was expected, and Lady Di liked to lean austeritywards on such occasions, Oliver Nash having made something of a circus, on his last visit, of harumphing at whatever he deemed unnecessary extravagance. His singling out of a print on her wall, a perfectly modest John Piper, still rankled. Today, then, the only hint of luxury was the plate of pastries neatly placed between the table's two utility holes. Raisin-studded, chocolate-sprinkled, icing-sugar frosted, the patisseries might have been assembled for a weekend supplement photo-shoot. A pile of napkins sat next to them. On a smaller table in the corner was a pot of filter coffee and a stack of takeaway cups. It had taken her ten minutes to get it all just right.

She had rinsed her hands in the nearby bathroom; stuffed the box the pastries came in into the nearest cupboard. By the time she heard the lift arrive, by the time the door opened, she was in one of the dreadful chairs; a notebook in front of her, a pen, still capped, lying in the ridge between its open pages.

"Diana. Ravishing as always."

"Oliver. Have you lost weight?"

It was an open secret that Nash had been attempting one diet or another for some time; long enough, indeed, for the cruel suggestion to be made that if he'd attempted them sequentially instead of all at once, one of them might have proved effective.

The look he gave her was not entirely free of suspicion. "I might have," he said.

"Oh, I'm positive. But please, sit. Sit. I've poured you a coffee."

He did so. "Rather spartan accommodation."

"Needs must, Oliver. We save the larger rooms for group sessions. Less wear and tear, and saves on heating, of course. I must apologise for this, by the way." She gestured at, without looking towards, the plate of pastries. "They're for the departmental gathering, I can't think why they've been brought in here. Somebody got their wires crossed."

"Hmph. Stretching the budget a little, wouldn't you say?"

"Oh, out of my own pocket. A little treat for the boys and girls on the hub. They work so hard."

"We're all very grateful."

His sandy hair had thinned in the last months, as if in

mockery of his attempts to diminish himself elsewhere, but his chins remained prominent. Fastidiously avoiding looking at the plate of pastries, he placed his hands on his paunch and fixed his gaze on Diana. "How's the ship? Come through choppy seas lately, haven't we?"

"If we'd wanted a quiet life, we'd have joined the fire brigade."

"Well, so long as we're all having fun." He seemed to realise that the placement of his hands emphasised the roundness of his stomach and shifted them to the tabletop, a more dynamic posture. "So. Snow White." He raised an eyebrow. "By the way, have I mentioned—"

"Everybody's mentioned."

"—what a ridiculous codename that is?"

"They're randomly assigned."

"I mean, what if it had been Goldilocks, for God's sake?"

"We might have had to re-roll the dice. But as things stand, we live with it."

"Do you ever feel that we've become slaves to the processes? Rather than their existing to facilitate our objectives?"

He had always been one for the arch observation, even when the observation in question was of unadorned banality.

"Let's save that for Wants and Needs, shall we?" she said, meaning the bi-monthly inter-departmental catch-up most people termed Whines & Niggles. "Snow White. You've received the request. There's no difficulty, surely?"

But Oliver Nash preferred being in the driving seat, and would take whatever damn route he chose.

"If memory serves," he said, "and it usually does, she was recruited by an older chap."

"John Bachelor."

"But here she is being handled by a new boy. How'd that come about?"

"It was felt that Bachelor wasn't up to the job."

"Why?"

"Because he wasn't up to the job."

"Ah. Got on your wrong side, did he?"

"I have no wrong sides, Oliver. I just find the occasional thorn in one, that's all."

Not that he had been particularly thorny, John Bachelor, since that would have required more character than he possessed. He was, rather, an also-ran; constantly sidelined throughout his career; ultimately parked on the milk round, the name given to the after-care service provided to pensioned-off assets. Bachelor's remit—which, in the last round of cuts, had been downgraded to "irregular"—involved ensuring that his charges remained secure, that no passes had been made in their direction; increasingly, that they were still alive and in possession of their marbles. They were Cold War footsoldiers, for the most part, who had risked their younger lives pilfering secrets for the West, and were eking out what time remained to them on Service pensions. A dying breed, in every sense.

But they had careers, or at least activities, to look back on with pride. John Bachelor, on the other hand, had little more than a scrapbook full of service-station receipts and the memory of a lone triumph: the recruitment of Snow White.

"And this new chap—Pynne? Richard Pynne?"

"He's not that new."

"Bet that name gave him sleepless nights as a boy."

"Luckily the Service isn't your old prep school. He'll be along in a moment. And—forgive me, I can't resist. I had to skip breakfast."

She helped herself to an almond croissant, took a dainty nibble from one end, and placed it carefully on a napkin.

"An extra five minutes on the treadmill," she said.

There was a knock on the door, and Richard Pynne appeared.

"You two haven't met," Taverner said. "Oliver Nash, Chair of Limitations, and one of the great and the good, as you won't need me to tell you, Richard. Oliver, this is Richard Pynne. Richard was Cambridge, I'm afraid, but you'll just have to forgive him."

"No great rivalry between Cambridge and the LSE, Diana, as I'm sure you remember all too well." Without getting up, he extended a hand, and Pynne shook it.

"A pleasure, sir."

"Help yourself to a pastry, Richard. Oliver was about to ask for a rundown on Snow White's request."

"Do you want me to . . ."

"In your own time."

Pynne sat. He was a large young man, and had dealt with a rapidly receding hairline by shaving his head from his teenage years; this, combined with thick-framed spectacles, lent him a geeky look which wasn't aided by his somewhat hesitant manner of speech. But he had a fully working brain, had scored highly on the agent-running scenarios put together across the river, and Snow White was a home-soil operation: low risk. Di Taverner didn't play favourites. She'd been known, though, to back winners. If Pynne handled his first joe without mishap he might find himself elevated above shift manager on the hub, his current role.

"Snow White's been having problems at BIS," he began.

"The Department for Business, Innovation and Skills," proclaimed Nash. "And I'd have a lot more confidence in its ability to handle all or any of those things if it could decide whether or not it was using a comma. What kind of problems?"

"Personnel."

"Personal?"

"*Onn*el," stressed Pynne. "Though it covers both, I suppose."

Nash looked at the pastries and sighed. "We'd better start at the beginning, I suppose."

In the beginning, Snow White—Hannah Weiss—was a civil servant, a fast-track graduate; indistinguishable from any other promising young thing hacking out a career in Whitehall's jungle, except that she'd been recruited at a young age by the BND—the Bundesnachrichtendienst; the German intelligence service. It was always useful to have agents in place, even when the spied-upon was nominally an ally. Especially when fault-lines were appearing the length and breadth of Europe. So far so what, as one of Pynne's generation might have ventured; this kind of low-level game-playing was part of the territory, and rarely resulted in more than the odd black eye, a bloodied nose. But this game was different. Hannah's "recruitment," it transpired, had been carried out without her awareness or consent: she had been no more than a name on a list fraudulently compiled by one Dieter Hess, himself a superannuated asset, one of the pensioners on John Bachelor's milk round. Hess, a shakedown of his cupboards had revealed after his death, had been supplementing his income by running a phantom network, his list consisting of shut-ins and lockaways, for each of whom the BND had been shelling out a small but regular income. Hannah Weiss alone had been living flesh, and unaware of her role in Hess's scheme. She was the one warm body in a league of ghosts.

It was John Bachelor who had uncovered Hess's deception, and Bachelor who'd come up with the idea of recruiting Hannah, then about to embark on her career in the Civil Service, and allowing the BND to continue thinking her its creature. It had been a bright idea, even Taverner allowed; the one creative spark of Bachelor's dimly lit career, but even then, the flint had been pure desperation. In the absence of his injury-time coup, Bachelor's neck would have been on the block. As it was, he'd scraped up enough credibility to hang onto his job, and Hannah Weiss, whom the BND thought in its employ, had been recruited by the Service, which, in return for low-grade Whitehall gossip, was building up a picture of how the BND ran its agents in the field.

Because it was always useful to have agents in place, even when the spied-upon was nominally an ally . . .

"Snow White's been doing well at BIS, but she feels, and I agree, that it's time for her to move on. There are offices where she'd be more valuable to the BND, which would mean, in return, that we'd get a peek at their more high-level practices. The more value they place on her, the more resources they'll expend."

"Yes, we get the basic picture," said Nash. He shot a look at Diana, who was taking another bite from her croissant, and seemed, in that moment, to be utterly transported. "But I thought we didn't want to get too ambitious. Maintain a solid career profile. We turn her into a shooting star, and put her in Number Ten or whatever, the BND'll smell a rat."

"Yes. But there've been, like I say, personnel problems, and this gives us an iron-clad reason for a switch."

"Tell."

"Snow White's manager has developed something of a crush on her."

"Oh, god."

"Late night phone calls, unwanted gifts, constant demands for one-on-one meetings which turn inappropriate. It's an unhappy situation."

"I can imagine. But this manager, can't he be—"

"She."

"Ah. Well, regardless, can't she be dealt with in-house? It's hardly unprecedented."

Diana Taverner said, "She could be. But, as Richard says, it provides us with an opportunity for a shuffling exercise. And we're not suggesting Snow White be moved to Number Ten. There is, though, one particular Minister whose office is expanding rapidly."

"The Brexit Secretary, I suppose."

"Precisely. A move there would be perfectly logical, given Snow White's background. German speakers are at a premium, I'd have thought."

Oliver Nash pressed a finger to his chin. "The Civil Service don't like it when we stir their pot."

"But there's a reason they're called servants."

"Not the most diplomatic of arguments." He looked at Pynne. "This suggestion came from Snow White herself?"

"She's keen to move. It's that or make an official complaint."

"Which would be a black mark against her," Diana said.

"Surely not," said Nash, with heavy sarcasm. His gaze shifted from one to the other, but snagged on the plate of pastries. It was to this he finally spoke: "Well, I suppose it'll all look part of the general churn. Tell her to make a formal transfer application. It'll be approved."

"Thank you, sir."

"Do take one of these, Richard. They're best fresh."

Richard Pynne thanked her too, took a raisin pastry, and left the room.

"There," said Lady Di. "Nice to get something done without umpteen follow-up meetings." She made a note in her book, then closed it. "So good of you to make the time."

"I hope young Pynne isn't taking a gamble with our Snow White just to cheer his CV up. Making himself look good is one thing. But if he blows her usefulness in the process, that'll be down to you."

"It's all down to me, Oliver. Always is. You know that."

"Yes, well. Sometimes it's better to stick than twist. There are dissenting voices, you know. An op like this, misinforming a friendly service, well, I know it comes under the heading fun and games, but it still costs. And that's without considering the blowback if the wheels come off. We rely on the BND's cooperation with counter-terrorism. All pulling together. What'll it look like if they find we've been yanking their chain?"

"They keep secrets, we keep secrets. That, as you put it, is where the fun and games comes in. And let's not forget the only reason we have Snow White is that the BND thought they were running a network on our soil. What's sauce for the goose goes well with the schnitzel, don't you think? More coffee?"

"I shouldn't."

But he pushed his cup towards her anyway.

Lady Di took it, crossed to the table in the corner, and poured him another cup. When she turned, he was reaching for a pastry.

She made sure not to be smiling on her return.

Solomon Dortmund said: "It was a drop."

"Well, I'm sure something was dropped—"

"It was a *drop*."

When he was excited, Solomon's Teutonic roots showed. This was partly, John Bachelor thought, a matter of his accent hardening; partly a whole-body shift, as if the ancient figure, balancing a bone china teacup on a bone china saucer and not

looking much more robust than either, had developed a sudden
steeliness within. He was, like most of those in Bachelor's care,
an ambassador from another era, one in which hardship was
familiar to young and old alike, and in which certainty was not
relinquished lightly. Solomon knew what he knew. He knew
he had seen a drop.

"She was a young thing, twenty-two, twenty-three."

John Bachelor mentally added ten years.

"Blonde and very pretty."

Of course, because all young women were very pretty. Even
the plain were pretty to the old, their youth a dazzling distraction.

"And he was a spook, John."

"You recognised him?"

"The type."

"But not the actual person."

"I'm telling you, I know what I saw."

He had seen a drop.

Bachelor sighed, without making much attempt to hide
it. He had much to sigh about. An icy wind was chasing up
and down the nearby Edgware Road, where frost patterned
the pavements. His left shoe was letting in damp, and before
long would be letting in everything else: the cold, the rain,
the inevitable snow. His overcoat was thinner than the
weather required; it was ten-fifteen, and already he wanted a
drink. Not needed, he noted gratefully, but wanted. He did
not have the shakes, and he was not hungover. But he wanted
a drink.

"Solly," he said. "This was Fischer's, on a Tuesday morning. It's a popular place, with a lot of traffic. Don't you think it possible that what you thought you saw was just some accidental interaction?"

"I don't think I saw anything," the old man said.

Result.

But Bachelor's hopes were no sooner formed than destroyed:

"I *know*. She passed him an envelope. She dropped a pile, he scooped them up. But one went into his coat pocket."

"A manila envelope."

"A manila envelope, yes. This is an important detail? Because you say it—"

"I'm just trying to establish the facts."

"—you say it as if it were an outlandish item for anyone to be in possession of, on a Tuesday morning. A manila envelope, yes. C5 size. You are familiar with the dimensions?"

Solomon held his hands just so.

"I'm familiar with the dimensions, yes."

"Good. It was a drop, John."

In trade terms, a passing on of information, instructions, *product*, in such a manner as to make it seem that nothing had occurred.

Bachelor had things to do; he had an agenda. Top of which was sorting his life out. Next was ensuring he had somewhere to sleep that night. It was likely that the first item would be held over indefinitely, but it was imperative that the second receive his full and immediate attention. And yet, if the milk round had taught John Bachelor anything, it was that when an old asset got his teeth into something, he wasn't going to let go until a dental mould had been cast.

"Okay," he said. "Okay. Have you a sheet of paper I can use? And a pen?"

"They don't supply you with these things?"

Bachelor had no idea whether they did or not. "They give us pens, but they're actually blowpipes. They're rubbish for writing with."

Solomon chuckled, because he was getting what he wanted, and rummaged in a drawer for a small notebook and a biro. "You can keep these," he said. "That way you will have a full record of your investigation."

I'm not an investigator, I'm a nursemaid. But they were past that point. "Young, blonde, very pretty." He wrote those words down. On the page, they looked strangely unconvincing. "Anything else?"

Solomon considered. "She was nicely dressed."

"Nicely dressed" went on a new line.

"And she was drinking tea."

After a brief internal struggle, Bachelor added this to his list.

Solomon shrugged. "By the time I knew to pay attention, she was already out of the door."

"What about the man?"

"He was about fifty, I would say, with brown hair greying at the temples. Clean-shaven. No spectacles. He wore a camel-hair coat over a dark suit, red tie. Patterned, with stripes. Black brogues, yellow socks. I noticed them particularly, John. A man who wears yellow socks is capable of anything."

"I've often thought so," Bachelor said, but only because Solomon was clearly awaiting a response.

"He ordered coffee and a slice of torte. He was right-handed, John. He held the fork in his right hand."

"Right-handed," Bachelor said, making the appropriate note in his book. The clock on the kitchen wall was making long-suffering progress towards twenty past the hour: with a bit of luck, he thought, he'd have grown old and died and be in his coffin by the time the half-hour struck.

"And he was reading the *Wall Street Journal*."

"He brought that with him?"

"No, he found it on a nearby seat."

"The one the girl had been using?"

"No."

"You're sure about that? Think carefully. It could be a crucial detail."

"I think you are playing the satirist now, John."

"Maybe a bit." He looked the older man in the eye. "Things like this don't happen any more. Drops in cafés? Once upon a time, sure, but nowadays? It's the twenty-first century." He'd nearly said the twentieth. "People don't do drops, they don't carry swordsticks."

"You think, instead, they deliver information by drone, or just text it to each other?" Solomon Dortmund shook his elderly head. "Or send it by email perhaps, so some teenager in Korea can post it on Twitter? No, John. There's a reason why people say the old ways are the best. It's because the old ways are the best."

"You're enjoying this, aren't you?"

"Enjoy? No. I am doing my duty, that is all."

"And what do you want me to do about it?"

Solomon shrugged. "Do, don't do, that is up to you. I was an asset, yes? That is the term you use. Well, maybe I'm not so useful any more, but I know what I saw and I've told you what I know. In the old days, that was enough. I pass the information on." He actually made a passing motion here, as if handing an invisible baby back to its mother. "What happens to it afterwards, that was never my concern."

Bachelor said, "Well, thanks for the notebook. It will come in handy."

"You haven't asked me if there is anything else."

"I'm sorry, Solomon. Was there anything else?"

"Yes. The man's name is Peter Kahlmann."

". . . Ah."

"Perhaps this information will help you trace him?"

"It can't hurt," said Bachelor, opening the notebook again.

The previous night had been unsatisfactory, to say the least; had been spent on a sofa not long enough, and not comfortable. His current lodgings were reaching the end of their natural lease, which is to say that after one week in the bed of the flat's owner—a former lover—he had spent two in the sitting room, and now the knell had been sounded. On arriving the previous evening, he had found his battered suitcase packed and ready, and it had only been by dint of special pleading, and reference to past shared happinesses—slight and long ago—that he had engineered one final sleepover, not that sleep had made an appearance. When dawn arrived, reluctantly poking its way past the curtains, Bachelor had greeted it with the spirit a condemned man might his breakfast: at least the wait was over, though there was nothing agreeable about what happened next.

And all that had brought him to this point: none of that was pretty either. Especially not the decision to cash in his pension and allow his former brother-in-law to invest the capital—no risk, no gain, John; have to speculate to accumu-late—a move intended to secure his financial future, which had been successful, but only in the sense that there was a certain security in knowing one's financial future was unlikely to waver from its present circumstance. And he had to give this much to the former brother-in-law: he'd finished the job his sister had started. When the lease on Bachelor's "studio flat"—yeah, right; put a bucket in the corner of a bedsit, and you could claim it was *en suite*—had come up for renewal last month, he'd been unable to scrape together the fees the letting company required for the burdensome task of doing sweet fuck all. And that was that. How could he possibly be homeless? He worked for Her Majesty's government. And just to put the icing on the cupcake, his job involved making sure that one-time foreign assets had a place to lay their head, and a cup of sweet tea waiting when they opened their eyes again. They called it the milk round. It might have been a better career choice being an actual fucking milkman, and that was taking into account that nobody had milk delivered any more. At least he'd have got to keep the apron; something to use as a pillow at night.

He was in a pub having these thoughts, having drunk the large scotch he hadn't needed but wanted, and now working on a second he hadn't thought he wanted but turned out to need. In front of him was the notebook Solomon had given him, and on a fresh page he was making a list of possible next moves. There were no other ex-lovers to be tapped up, not if he valued his genitals. *Hotel*, he'd already crossed out. His credit cards had been thrashed to within an inch of their lives; they'd combust in the daylight like vampires. *Estate agents* he'd also scored through. The amount of capital you needed to set yourself up in a flat, a bedsit, a vacant stretch of corridor in London, was so far beyond a joke it had reached the other side and become funny again. How did anyone manage this? There was a good reason, he now understood, why unhappy marriages survived, and it was this: an unhappy marriage at least had two people supporting it. Once you cut yourself loose, disinvested from the marital property, you could either look forward to a life way down on the first rung or move to, I don't know, the fucking North.

But let's not get too wrapped up in self-pity, John. Worse comes to worst, you can sleep in your car.

Bachelor sighed and made inroads on his drink. At the top of this downward spiral was work, and the downgrading of his role to "irregular," which was HR for part-time. A three-day week, with concomitant drop in salary: You won't mind, will

you, John? Look on it as a toe in the waters of retirement . . .
He'd be better off being one of his own charges. Take Solomon
Dortmund. Dortmund was a million years old, sure, and had
seen rough times, and it wasn't like Bachelor begrudged him
safe harbour, but still: he had that little flat, and a pension to
keep him in coffee and cake. There'd been a moment an hour
ago when he'd nearly asked Solomon the favour: a place to kip
for a night or two. Just until he worked out something permanent. But he was glad he hadn't. Not that he thought the old
man would have refused him. But Bachelor couldn't have borne
his pity.

Feisty old bugger, though.

"I waited until he'd left," Solomon had said. "There is always
something to do on the High Street. You know the marvelous
bookshop?"

"Everyone does."

"And then I returned and had a word with the waiter. They
all know me there."

"And they knew your man? By name?"

"He is a regular. Once or twice, he has made a booking. So
yes, the waiter knew his name just as he knew mine."

"And was happy to tell you?"

"I said I thought I recognised him, but too late to say hello.
A nephew of an old friend I was anxious to be in touch with."
Solomon had given an odd little smile, half pride, half regret.
"It is not difficult to pretend to be a confused old man. A
harmless, confused old man."

Bachelor had said, "You're a piece of work, Solly. Okay, I'll raise this back at the Park. See what they can do with the name."

And now he flicked back a page and looked again: Peter Kahlmann. German-sounding. It meant nothing, and the thought of turning up at Regent's Park and asking for a trace to be run was kind of funny; beyond satire, actually. John Bachelor wasn't welcome round Regent's Park. Along with the irregular status went a degree of autonomy; which meant, in essence, that nobody gave a damn about his work. The milk round had a built-in obsolescence; five years, give or take, and his charges would be in their graves. For now, he made a written report once a month, unless an emergency happened—death or hospitalisation—and kept well clear until summoned. And this non-status was largely down to the Hannah Weiss affair.

Hannah should have been a turning point. He'd recruited her, for God's sake; had made what might have been a career-ending fiasco a small but nonetheless decorative coup, giving the Park a channel into the BND: a friendly Service, sure, but you didn't have to be in John Bachelor's straits to understand what friendship was worth when the chips were down. And given all that had happened since—Brexit, he meant—Christ: that young lady was worth her weight in rubies. And it had all been down to him, his idea, his trade-craft, so when he'd learned he wouldn't be running her—seriously, John? Agent-running? You don't think that's a little out of your league?—he'd got shirty, he supposed; had become a little boisterous. Truth be told, he might have had a drink or two. Anyway, long story short, he'd been escorted from the premises, and when the Dogs escorted you from Regent's Park, trust this: you knew you'd been escorted. He might have lost his job altogether if they could have been bothered to find a replacement. As it was, the one morsel he'd picked up on the grapevine was that Snow White, which was what they were calling her now, had been farmed out to Lady Di's latest favourite: one Richard Pynne, if you could believe that. Dick the Prick. You had to wonder what some parents thought they were doing.

Bachelor yawned, his broken night catching up with him. Through the pub window he could see it trying to snow; the air had a pent-up solid grey weight to it, like a vault. If he had to spend the night in the car, currently Plan A by default, there was a strong likelihood he'd freeze to death, and while he'd heard there were worse ways to go, he didn't want to run a consumer test. Perhaps he should rethink approaching Solomon . . . Pity was tough to bear, but grief would be worse, even if he weren't around to witness it. But if so, he'd have to either come up with a story as to why he'd got nowhere tracing Peter Kahlmann or, in fact, try tracing Peter Kahlmann. It occurred to him that of the two options, the latter required less effort. He checked his watch. Still shy of noon, which gave him a little wiggle room. Okay, he thought. Let's try tracing Peter Kahlmann. If he'd got nowhere by three, he'd apply himself to more urgent matters.

And he did, as it happened, have an idea where to start.

• • •

A coffee shop just off Piccadilly Circus: a posh one where they gave you a chocolate with your coffee, but placed it too close to your cup, so it half-melted before reaching the table.

Hannah Weiss didn't mind. There was something decadent about melting chocolate; the way it coated your tongue. Just so long as you didn't get it on your fingers or clothes.

Richard Pynne said, "So it'll go through like you asked. Make your transfer application. You don't have to mention the stalking thing. It'll be expedited end of next week at the latest."

"That's great, Richard. Thank you."

She'd enjoyed working at BIS, but it was time for a change. If Richard hadn't come through, "the stalking thing," as he'd put it, would probably have done the trick, but it was as well she hadn't had to go down that route. Julia, her line manager, would be horrified at the accusation; though of all the people who'd inevitably become involved, Julia would be easiest to convince of her own guilt. There was a certain kind of PC mindset which was never far away from eating itself. But more problematic would be being noticed for the wrong thing. Like all large organisations, the Civil Service hoisted flags about how its staff should report wrongdoing, but if you actually did so, your card was marked for life. It was hard not to feel aggrieved about that, even if the reported wrongdoing was fabricated.

Pynne said, "I actually had a pastry earlier. Not sure I want a chocolate now."

Because he was expecting her to, she said, "Well, if you don't . . ."

He grinned and turned his saucer round so the chocolate was nearest her. Using finger and thumb, she popped it into her mouth whole. Richard watched the process, his grin flickering.

"You're okay with us meeting here?"

"Sure. I'll have to be back in the office in twenty minutes though."

"That's okay. I just wanted to pass on the good news."

They were of an age, or at least, he wasn't so much older that it looked unusual, the pair of them meeting for coffee. Nobody observing would have to make up a story to fit; they were just pals, that was all. He'd suggested, of course—back when they were building this legend—that he be an ex-boyfriend; still close, maybe on/off. And she'd given it genuine thought, but only for the half-second it took to reject it. The alacrity with which he'd agreed that it wasn't, after all, a great idea had amused her, but she'd taken care to keep that hidden. On paper he was her handler, and it was all round best if he thought that was the case in the real world too.

She supposed, if she were more important to the Park, they'd have given her someone with more experience; a father figure, someone like the man who'd recruited her in the first place. Pynne, though, was learning the game as much as she was; they were each other's starter partners, or that was the idea. A fun-and-games op; blowing smoke in a friendly Agency's eyes, just to show they could, though European Rules had changed in the years since Hannah's recruitment, and if nobody was expecting hostilities to break out, a certain amount of tetchiness was on the cards. So maybe her value to the Park was on an upward trajectory, but even so, she wouldn't be assigned a new handler now. It didn't really matter. The fact was, Hannah Weiss had been playing this game for a lot longer than Richard Pynne. And the handler the BND had matched her with had a lot more field savvy; but then, he knew Hannah was a triple, working for the BND, while the Park thought she was a double, working for the Park.

Maybe everyone would sit down and have a good laugh about all of this one day, but for the moment, it suited her real bosses that she be transferred to the office handling Brexit negotiations. It wasn't the world's biggest secret that Britain had been handling these discussions with the grace and aplomb of a rabbit hiding a magician in its hat, but, on the slim chance that somebody had a masterplan up their sleeve, the BND wouldn't have minded a peek.

"So . . . Everything else all right?"

Hannah sipped her coffee, looked Richard Pynne directly in the eye, and said, "Yes. Yes, all fine."

He nodded, as if he'd just managed a successful debriefing. It was hard not to compare his treatment of her with that of Martin, who sometimes insisted on clandestine handovers in public places—the old ways are the best, Hannah; you have to learn how to do things the hard way; this is how we do a *drop*, Hannah; learn this now, it may someday save your life—and other times spirited her away for the evening; one of the brasher clubs round Covent Garden, where up-and-coming media types mingle with new-breed business whizzkids. Those evenings, they'd drink champagne cocktails, like a September/ May romance in the making, and his interrogation of her life was a lot less timid than Richard Pynne's. What about lovers, Hannah; fucking anybody useful? You don't have to say if you don't want to. I'll find out anyway. But she didn't mind telling him. When they were together, she didn't have to hide who she was. And not hiding who she was included letting him know how much she enjoyed hiding who she was; how much she enjoyed playing these games in public. Because that's what it was, so far; a fun-and-games op in one of the world's big cities. How could she not be enjoying herself?

"But don't ever forget, Hannah, that if they catch you, they'll put you in prison. That's when the fun stops, are you receiving me?"

Loud and clear, Martin. Loud and clear.

Now she said to Richard Pynne, "I'll put my application in this afternoon. The sooner the better, yes?"

"Good girl."

She finished her coffee, and smiled sweetly. "Richard? Don't get carried away. I'm not your good girl."

"Sorry. Sorry—"

"Richard? You have to learn when I'm teasing."

"Sorry—"

And she left him there, to settle their bill; not looking back from the cold pavement to his blurred face behind the plate glass window, like a woman who's just told her Labrador to stay, and won't test his mettle by flashing him kindness.

• • •

At Regent's Park the weather, to no one's surprise, was much the same as elsewhere in London; the skies sea-grey, the air chill, and packed with the promise of snow.

John Bachelor was having conversation with a guardian of the gate, who in this particular instance was seated at a desk in the lobby. "You're not expected," she was telling him, something he was already aware of.

"I know," he said. "That's what 'without appointment' means. But I'm not meeting with anyone, I just need to do some research."

"You should still book in ahead."

He swallowed the responses which, in a better life, he'd have had the freedom to deliver, and managed a watery smile. "I know, I know. Mea culpa. But my plans for the day have gone skew-whiff, and this is the one chance I have at redeeming the hour."

His plans for the day had obviously involved shaving and putting a clean shirt on, the woman's non-spoken reply spelled out. Because those things hadn't happened either. But she ran his name and ID card through her scanner anyway, and evidently didn't come up with any kill-or-capture-on-sight instructions. "It says you're in good standing," she said, with a touch too much scepticism for Bachelor's liking. "But I'd rather see your name on the roster."

All or nothing.

"You want me to give Diana a ring?" He produced his mobile phone. "Sorry, I mean Ms. Taverner. I could call her and she can put you straight."

For a horrible second he thought she was about to call his bluff, but the moment passed; gave him a cheery wave, he liked to think, on its way through the door. She did something on her keyboard, and a printer buzzed. Retrieving its product, peeling a label from the sheet, she clipped it onto a lanyard. "That's a two-hour pass," she told him. "One second over, I send in the Dogs."

"Thank you."

"Have a nice visit."

Seriously, he thought, passing through the detectors and heading for the staircase; seriously: Checkpoint Charlie must have been more fun, back in the old days. Not that he'd actually been there. On the other hand he knew what it was, and wouldn't mistake it for a Twitter handle.

He took the lift and headed for the library. He didn't have an appointment, it was true, because an appointment would have appeared on someone's calendar, and anything documented in the Park carried the potential for blowback of one sort or another. Bachelor's standing might be "good," as the guardian of the gate had reluctantly verified, but "good" simply meant he wasn't currently on a kill-list. If he actually did bump into Di Taverner, she might have him dropped down a lift shaft just for the practice. So no, no actual appointment, but he had rung ahead and made contact with one of the locals; asked if they could have a quick chat, off the books. In the library. If the local was around, that was.

He was.

They still called it the library, but there weren't books here

any longer, only desks with cables for charging laptops. Bachelor settled in the corner furthest from the door, draped his
coat on a chair, then went and fetched a cup of coffee from the
dispenser, on his way back suffering a glimpse of a future that
awaited him, one in which he haunted waiting rooms and
libraries, anywhere he might sit in the warmth for ten minutes
before being asked to move on. How had it come to this? What
had happened to his life? He made a panicky noise out loud,
a peculiar little *eck*-sound, which he immediately repeated
consciously, turning it into a cough halfway through. But there
was only one other person in the room, a middle-aged woman
focused on her screen; she had earplugs in, and didn't glance
his way.

At his table, he warmed his hands on the plastic cup. He
didn't have his laptop—he'd left it in his car; a disciplinary
offence, come to think of it—so opened his notebook and
pretended to study his own words of wisdom. He must have
looked like an illustration of how he felt: an analogue man in
a digital world. No wonder it was leaving him behind so
quickly. But others managed. Look at Solomon. Bachelor
thought again of that cosy flat, its busy bookshelves, the active
chessboard indicating Solomon's continuing engagement in
struggle, even an artificial one, played out with himself. By any
current reckoning, Solomon was of no account; part of the last
century's flotsam, unless it was jetsam; discarded by a now-uni-
fied state, washed up onto an island that had lately reasserted
its insularity. But he still felt himself part of the game, enough
to alert Bachelor that he'd thought he'd seen a drop. No,

Bachelor corrected himself; Solly *knew* what he'd seen. He might have been wrong, but that was barely relevant. Solomon knew.

The name Peter Kahlmann stared up at Bachelor from the notebook in front of him.

So okay, it was true that he had designs on Solomon's sofa; on having somewhere to sleep that wasn't the back seat of his own car. But that didn't mean he couldn't pursue the trail in front of him to the best of his careworn abilities—he wasn't, when you got down to it, acting under false pretences. He was, in fact, acting under genuine pretences, and if in some eyes that might seem worse, it was the best he could manage in the circumstances.

"Bachelor?"

He started, alarmed that he'd been found out.

"It is you, right?"

And he admitted that indeed it was.

"Alec?" was how Bachelor had greeted him the first time they met. "Do I detect a touch of Scots?"

"It's Lech," Alec said. "And no, I'm not one of the Scottish Wicinskis. But good catch."

So yes, Alec Wicinski, born Lech, to parents themselves UK citizens, but both offspring of Poles who'd settled here during the war; named by his mother for the hero of the hour, Lech Wałęsa, which proved such a burden to the young Lech throughout a turbulent school career that he reinvented himself at

University: Alec, good proper name, nothing off the wall about it. He'd since come to semi-regret the change, and now answered to both, depending on who was addressing him. That he had two names—two covers, both real—amused him. Made him feel more a spy than his Service card did.

Which stated, when run through a scanner, that Alec Wicinski was an analyst, Ops division, which meant he worked on the hub, except for those rare occasions when he sat in the back of a van, watching other people kick doors down. Afterwards, he'd be who you went to to find out why the door hadn't come off its hinges first kick, or where the stuff you'd expected to find behind it might be now. Where John Bachelor had encountered him had been at the funeral of an ancient asset, who'd been a friend of Alec's grandfather, unless he'd been the grandfather of Alec's friend. Bachelor was hazy on the details, having launched himself wholeheartedly into the inevitable wake, but he'd made a point of scratching Wicinski's name on the wall of his memory cave. You never knew when a contact at the Park would come in handy.

Alec sat, and shook his head when Bachelor suggested coffee. "You have a name that might interest me?"

"It came through one of my people," Bachelor told him. Having people lent him weight, he thought. "Might be something, might be nothing."

"Are we currently in a movie?"

". . . What?"

"It just sounds like movie dialogue, that's all. 'Might be something, might be nothing.' I process information, John. It is John, right?" It is. "So, all information's either useful or it's not. But none of it's nothing. What's the name?"

"Peter Kahlmann," Bachelor said.

"And what's the context?"

Bachelor said, "One of my people, I look after retired assets, I think I told you that, one of my people thought he saw him making a drop. Or taking a drop, rather."

"A drop?"

"An exchange of some sort. A package. An envelope. Done surreptitiously in a public place."

"Sounds kind of old school."

"That's what I thought."

"I didn't know they even did that any more. Whoever they are." Alec scratched his head. He had thick dark curls. "And even if they did, that doesn't make it our business. Could be anything. Could be drugs."

"A lot of drug money goes places where it becomes our business," Bachelor said.

"Yeah, I know. Just thinking out loud. Who's the asset?"

"An old boy, one of our pensioners."

"Behind the curtain?"

"Back in the day, yes."

Alec nodded. The eyes behind his glasses were dark, but lively. "And where did he see what he says he saw? And where did the name come from?"

Bachelor ran through it all, start to finish. He didn't hide what he thought was possible: that Solomon Dortmund, who was sharp but ancient, might have witnessed an innocent stumble. But he didn't hide, either, that Solomon had seen such games played for real; that he'd played them himself, in places where, when you were caught, they didn't just make you sit out the next round.

"So why aren't you going through channels?" Alec said, when he'd finished.

". . . Channels?"

"If this is real, and not just an old man's mistake, it should go on the record. You know how this works. There's a reason we keep intel on file. It's so we can see the bigger picture. This Kahlmann, somewhere down the line, if he turns out to be planning an acid-attack on the PM's hairdresser, I don't want to be the one sticking my hand up and saying, oh yeah, we had a line on him, but it didn't go through channels so nobody noticed."

Bachelor, freewheeling, said, "If it's a mistake, it's a mark against Solly. And you're right, he's an old man. They decide he's being a nuisance, they might pack him off to one of those homes they have, where you're not allowed more possessions than'll fit in your locker, and everyone gathers in the home room for an afternoon sing-song. It'd kill him."

"But if he's seeing things that don't really happen, maybe one of those places is where he ought to be."

"Do you have parents, Alec?"

"Please. Don't play that card."

"It's the only one I've got."

Alec Wicinski scowled, then stared for a moment or two at Bachelor's coffee cup. Then said, "Okay, here's what I'll do. I'll run the name through the records, see if it rings any bells. And if it does I'll let you know, and then you can take it through official channels, okay?"

"Thanks, Alec."

"But don't tell anyone I made a pass at it first. We're not supposed do favours. Not even for people we don't actually know, but just bumped into at a funeral."

"Hell of a funeral, though," Bachelor said.

Alec grinned. "It was," he said. "It was a hell of a funeral."

Afterwards, Bachelor lingered in the library, drinking two more cups of coffee, then—inevitably—had to take himself off to find the nearest toilet. And as he did so, he had that sense of foreboding again; a glimpse of a life spent looking for facilities he could use. Brushing his teeth in car park lavatories. Lurking near department store bathrooms, trying to look like a customer.

For the first ever time, it struck him: if this was what he had to look forward to, should he maybe just bow out?

It wasn't a moment of illumination; more a taking-on-board of something found at the back of his mind. Not *the* answer, necessarily, because something might turn up, but still: a way out of his current predicament; a means of avoiding the humiliations piling up ahead, like a roadblock designed by Kafka. He could simply pull the switch. The thought didn't fill him with a sense of triumph, but the fact that it didn't fill him with dread struck the deeper chord. It was said that people who talked about killing themselves never actually did so. And he wondered if those people who did had had moments similar to this one; whether their first inkling that that big word, suicide, had specific relevance to themselves arrived not hand-in-hand with calamity but during an ordinary day; and whether it had felt to them, as it did to him, like opening an envelope addressed to The Occupier, and finding their own name on the letter within.

And then he shuddered and filed such thoughts away, though he knew that a seal had been broken, and that he'd be forced to dip into this dark jar again in the future, probably at night.

There was a bathroom down the corridor. After he'd peed, while he was washing his hands, someone else entered, and Bachelor spoke almost without intending to. "Do they still have showers on this floor? I pulled an all-nighter. I could really do with cleaning up."

"Next floor down," he was told.

"Thanks."

Next floor down was easily found. The building's geography was coming back to him as he wandered: showers, yes, and wasn't this where the bunking-down rooms were, where staff could crash when they were under the hammer? In the shower room were cupboards with towels, and even overnight kits: toothpaste, toothbrush, soap. He stayed under water as hot as he could manage until his skin grew lobster-pink. Then brushed his teeth and dressed again.

He was working on automatic now. It barely constituted a

plan. Back in the corridor he made his way towards the bed-rooms. None were in use. He chose one, let himself in, and locked the door behind him. The room wasn't much bigger than the single bed it contained, but that was all he was inter-ested in. He undressed again, climbed into the bed, and when he flipped the light switch, the room became totally dark; a chamber deaf to noise and blind to light. For the first time in weeks, Bachelor felt alone and completely secure. Within minutes he slept, and dreamed about nothing.

It didn't do to be a man of habit, so Martin Kreutzmer wasn't: varying the routes he took to work; shuffling the bars he fre-quented, and the shops he patronised with no discernible brand loyalty. Some days he wore a suit; others, he dressed like a student. But he contained multitudes, obviously—he was a handler, an agent-runner, and handlers are all things to all joes—so it wasn't surprising that some of his identities took a less stringent attitude: an identity hardly counted as such if it couldn't be broken down into lists. Likes/dislikes, favourite haunts, top ten movies. So when he was being Peter Kahlmann, he did the things Peter Kahlmann liked to do, one of which was visit Fischer's every so often, because even agent runners enjoy a taste of the homeland now and again. He'd barely sat, barely glanced at the menu, when the waiter was asking him, "Did your uncle's friend get in touch?"

"...I'm sorry?"

"Mr. Dortmund. One of our regulars, I'm surprised you've

not crossed paths before. Though you're not usually here in the mornings, like he is."

"Could you start at the beginning, please?"

Afterwards, he enjoyed his coffee break, to all outward appearance unbothered by the exchange: Yes, now he remembered; old Mr. Dortmund—Solly, that was it—had indeed been in touch, and yes, it was lovely to hear from someone who'd known Uncle Hans in the Old Days. Not many of that generation left. And yes, thank you, a slice of that delicious torte: What harm could it do? He gazed benignly round, and cursed inwardly. What had he done to attract the attention of an old man? There was only one answer: the drop. If the old man had noticed this, he must have been in the game himself. And if he'd taken it upon himself to establish Martin's—Peter's—identity, maybe he still was. Maybe he still was.

Martin blamed himself. Here on friendly ground—more or less—his duties were mostly administrative, and the bulk of his time was spent schmoozing compatriot bankers and businessmen, who thought him something to do with the Embassy. Hannah Weiss was his only active agent, and yes, he'd made a game of his dealings with her, partly so she could learn how things were done properly; partly because he got bored otherwise. Lately, though, the ground had been shifting. European boundaries were being resurrected; the collapse of the Union couldn't be ruled out. There were those who said it couldn't happen, and those who couldn't believe it hadn't happened yet, and as far as Martin was aware, similar groups of people had said similar things about the Wall, both when it went up and when it came down again. It wasn't like the Cold War was about to be redeclared. But still, Hannah's value as an agent could only increase in the future. It was time to stop playing games.

As for the here and now, the report she'd passed him, here in Fischer's, indicated that all was going to plan. Her move from BIS to the Brexit Secretary's office was in the bag. With that jump, her value to the BND would increase fivefold; no longer an amusing sideline, she'd be a genuine source of useful data. But even if that weren't so, he chided himself, he remained at fault for putting her in harm's way. Even amusing sidelines had to be taken seriously. Practising old-school spycraft on the streets of London was one thing; getting spotted doing it was another. Hannah's career to date might have been little more than a joke one Service was playing on another, but they wouldn't simply waggle a finger in her face if she was caught. And whoever this Solomon Dortmund was, he looked set to make that happen, if he hadn't done so already.

Caught by sudden urgency, Martin Kreutzmer paid and left. In the old days, he'd have had to head back to his office and set research wheels in motion; track this fox Dortmund to his den. But these days you could do all that on the move, which is exactly what Martin did, striding along the High Street, coat collar up against the wind; one glove dangling by a fingertip from his teeth as he squeezed information from his phone.

• • •

Back in the Park, Alec Wicinski was doing much the same
thing.

Dark curly hair; glasses half the time; a need to shave twice
a day, though needs didn't always must in his case. Alec was a
tie-wearer, a reader, and a walker; not one for hill and field or
coastal path, but a pounder of city streets, his usual cure for the
bouts of insomnia that plagued him being to march through
London after-hours. His fiancée, Sara, joked that she'd picked
him up on a street corner in the middle of the night. They'd
actually met through a mutual friend, the old-fashioned way.
Alec once worked out that they were the only engaged couple
he knew who hadn't met online, and still wasn't sure whether
to be surprised by that, and if so, why.

Alec, as noted, was an analyst, and oppo research his spe-
cialist subject, "oppo" being granted broad definition these
days. The lines were wavier than they used to be, old rivalries
nearer the surface, and anyone who wasn't spying for us was
spying on us. That, at least, was the motto on the hub, where
whistleblowing was the worst of crimes. There was something
about an enemy pretending to be a friend, or a friend pretending to be an enemy, that could be lived with; but that either
kind could pretend to have a conscience was a play too far. The
boys and girls on the hub knew things could get murky, and
that dirty truths had to be buried deep to keep the soil fertile;
dragging them to the surface did nobody good. Lech understood this, and any dirty truths he uncovered that he was

unhappy about he shelved in an attic corner of his mind, alongside his memories of his grandfathers' generation; those who'd fled Poland before the occupation, and fought their war under foreign skies. Back then, there was no doubting who the enemy was. Things were black or they were white, and even when they weren't—when there was shading round the edges— you acted as if they were, because that was what life during wartime was like, especially when your country was overrun. You'd picked your side. You didn't get to dictate strategy.

Those foreign skies were his own now, but his Polish extraction—at least, he'd always assumed that's what it was, though maybe it was some individual quirk all his own—kept history fresher in his mind than most of his colleagues managed. And whereas the general attitude was that right would ultimately triumph, something in Lech's bones sang of doom, or whispered along with the chorus: he was in his job to prevent bad things happening, but couldn't entirely suppress the fear that sooner or later he'd fail, that they'd all fail, that their home skies would look down on cataclysm. His grandfathers had taught him this much: that if you expected things to get worse, history would generally see you all right. Not that he'd be thanked for broadcasting this round the office.

For the moment, though, he did what he could.

Peter Kahlmann. Alec had a few spelling variations up his sleeve, but that was the version he entered first, running a multiple-site search on a number of Service engines: foreign operatives, British civilians, persons of interest of any nationality. The breadth meant he couldn't expect a response any

time soon, so he let his laptop get on with it, while he busied
himself with a report on a recent op in the Midlands—sev-
enteen arrests, and an armed assault on Birmingham
International scotched at the planning stage. Preventing bad
things happening: one for our side, he thought, and sup-
pressed the inevitable comeback from his mental gremlin,
Nobody wins all the time.

Outside, it was starting to snow.

The flat was off Edgware Road, in a pleasant block with
railinged-off basement areas, almost all of which contained an
army of terracotta pots with small, neatly sculpted evergreens
standing sentry. Upper storeys boasted windowboxes on most
of the sills. At this time of year, they were little more than a
gardener's memento mori; the odd scrappy fighter among them
battling the winter, but most standing fallow, waiting the bad
months out. As if in vindication of their decision, it started to
snow as Martin Kreutzmer approached; big chunky flakes
drifting lazily down, the way Christmas card artists prefer, and
a nice change from the dirty sleet London usually conjured up.

Outwardly, the block maintained the appearance of a row
of houses, each with its own front door up a flight of stone
steps. Sets of doorbells were fixed to the brickwork, labelled
by name, and Martin had no trouble finding the one he was
after: No. 36, Flat 5. He looked up and down the road. There
were few people, and the only moving traffic was out of sight:
shunting up and down Edgware Road. All he was doing, he

told himself, was checking out the opposition. There remained the possibility that Solomon Dortmund was exactly who he said he was: a friend of Martin's uncle. Except Martin didn't have any uncles, and even if he did, they wouldn't have any friends. So maybe Solomon Dortmund was in play, which meant Martin had to find out who was pulling his strings. For his own part, he was fireproof: the worst the British Secret Service could do to him was purse its lips in his direction. But if Hannah was blown, he'd have to put her on the next flight out of the country.

First things first: Martin rang the bell. Old people respond to doorbells; ingrained politeness, combined with a sense of need: the need to show visitors they were up and dressed, mobile, *compos mentis*. It was possible he was projecting. Anyway, Solomon Dortmund didn't answer his bell, meaning the odds were he was out, which gave Martin a whole new set of options: act as if the worst had happened, and pull Hannah's rip-cord, or carry on digging in case the whole thing turned out to be an old man's brainfart. When in doubt, he thought, secure your joe; that was the bedrock of agent-running. Back home they'd throw their hands up and ask if he was getting scaredy-cat in age, but screw that: they weren't the ones who'd be carted off in a Black Maria if it all went wrong. He wasn't about to gamble Hannah's future just to keep the bean counters happy, so he was pulling the cord, and that was the decision he'd come to as the door opened and an old woman emerged, a dog in her arms, a shopping basket looped through one of them too. "You are *such* a nuisance,"

she was saying, and Martin could only presume she was
addressing the dog. Confirmation arrived when she looked
him directly in the eye. "He is *such* a nuisance."

"But a fine fellow all the same," he told her. "Let me get
that for you." Meaning the door, which he held while she
made her slow way through: dog, shopping basket, a walking
stick too, it turned out. "Can I see you down the steps?"

"That would be kind."

"Let me just fix this," he said. "Don't want to have to
disturb anyone again." He lay his gloves down to prevent
the door shutting and then, to forestall any interrogation as
to who he was visiting, and what the nature of his business
was, kept up an unbroken commentary on dogs he had
known while helping his companion to the pavement: was
he one for chasing squirrels? Martin himself had heard that
terriers were the very devil for squirrels; had known one
personally, hand on heart, that had learned to climb trees.
Sweetest dog in the world, that quirk apart. Would rescue
ducklings, and escort lost fledglings back to their nests, but
squirrels: that dog had an issue with squirrels. By the time
all was done, and she was heading off towards Marks &
Spencer, Martin had almost convinced himself he'd known
her years, such was the degree of fondness with which she
took her leave. Dear boy. He headed back up the steps,
retrieved his gloves, and closed the door behind him. Solomon Dortmund: Flat 5. Two flights up.

Must be a game old bird right enough, Martin thought,
as proud of his command of English idiom as he was of his

ability to get up the stairs without losing breath. He'd found
no images of Solomon Dortmund on his quick trawl through
the ether, but the one in his mind had the old man a robin:
bright of eye and twice as perky, hopping up and down these
stairs twice a day, for all he was eighty. Ninety? And here
was his door, and Martin rapped on it, and again there was
no response. This wasn't great tradecraft, but sometimes you
rode your luck. Plan an operation, and it took you weeks.
Grab an opportunity, and you could be back in your foxhole
by teatime, mission accomplished. It was a good solid door,
and a top-hole lock. There were spies out there, good and
bad, who could find their way through a locked door, but
Martin Kreutzmer wasn't one of them. He'd read a few
books, though. He ran a hand along the top of the door-
frame and found nothing, then bent to the welcome mat.
Who kept a welcome mat outside their front door? An old
person. Or maybe just a hospitable person, he amended, and
lifted the mat and found the spare key carefully taped to the
underside. Solomon, Solomon, he thought. Thank you for
that. He heard a noise downstairs and froze, but the noise—a
door opening and closing—was followed by its own echo:
someone going out onto the street. He looked at the key.
Yes or no? He'd not have a better chance. Three minutes
tops, he told himself. Just to find out who this geezer—this
robin—thinks he is.

And he let himself into the flat.

· · ·

And here was the snow they'd been expecting, thought Solomon; a few little flurries to start with, to make everyone sentimental about how pretty London looked with its edges rounded, and then more intently, more seriously; this was snow with a job to do, snow that would cause everything to grind to a halt: buses and taxis, the underground, the people, the shops, the law, the government. All these years gone by, and he still didn't know what it was with the British and snow. Pull on your boots, wear gloves, spread a little salt and put shovels in the hands of the right people: What was so difficult about that? But no, let any kind of weather turn up looking grim and the country went into shock. But ah well, he thought; ah well, at least he'd had the sense to notice which way the wind was blowing. So here he was, loaded shopping bags in each hand, and if the snow meant he was confined to his flat for a week, while the oafs on the Council ran round like headless chickens, wondering what the white stuff was and how to make it go away again, at least he wouldn't be wondering where his next tin of sardines was coming from, or be forced to re-use coffee grounds. That had happened before.

He had to put all his bags down to find his doorkeys. They were never in the pocket you'd put them in; that was something else a long life had taught him, that keys were determined to drive you out of your mind, but ah, here they were, and he could perhaps fish them out without removing his gloves, but no, that wasn't going to happen: off come the gloves, Solomon. Off come the gloves, as if he were about to enter battle, when in fact his day's campaign was over: he had his shopping, he had his keys—yes, there they were, plain as daylight in his hand—and now all he had to do was carry this shopping up two flights of stairs and he could settle down in his chair while the outside world did its worst.

The door was open, the shopping bags lugged over the threshold, the door was closed again, the light was on. Solomon felt dizzy when this was completed, and was breathing hard. Nonsense to suggest that a little exertion was too much for him; but on the other hand, on the other hand. He had outlived everyone he had ever loved, and while he viewed a number of those still breathing with affection, he wouldn't miss them when he was gone as much as he'd delight in the company of those he'd be joining. And it was often the case, he reflected, that you had such thoughts at the bottom of a staircase. Once you'd reached the top, there were more immediate things to dwell on, such as the contents of his shopping bags. Tins of sardines and necessary pints of milk apart, a few treats had been included. An old man doesn't need chocolate. But an old man has every right to a few things he doesn't need, when the snow outside is falling hard, and no telling when he'd next make it to Fischer's. The dizziness passed, and he chuckled. What were a few more flights of stairs? His life so far, he'd long lost count of how many stairs he'd climbed. Everyone did, after the first few.

But here he was now, up both flights, and his front door awaiting him. Again, there was the problem with the keys, which turned up in the wrong pocket, second time of looking. A sorry business, this growing older every day. But moments

later he was home; in his own warm flat where all his possessions waited, his comfortable chair, his small library, his
slippers, his life. He closed the door, and would have taken
his bags through to the kitchen had something not struck
him: not a thought, not a sound, a smell; a stranger's smell—
there had been, possibly still was, someone in his flat who
should not be there; someone who carried, as Solomon did, his
own odour: sweat, soap, all the undefinables we muster along
the way. Solomon's heart was hammering now; his breathing
rapid. Were they still here? The door had been locked, was
unbroken; a skilled burglar could enter through a window, but
not without being seen from the street, surely, at this time of
day? He sniffed deliberately, but the smell had been erased by
odours from his shopping bags: the fresh bread, the fruit, the
minced lamb, the cheese—the cheese? Was that what had
snagged his attention, the urgent clamouring of a goat's cheese?
He reached out for the nearest shopping bag and raised it
head-high, sniffed again. Ha! Goat's cheese! He had heard
many tales of old men frightened by their shadows, but this—
this!—he would not be living this down soon, even if it
remained his closely guarded secret, which it would. It would.

Solomon carried the bags to the kitchen then returned to
the door, removed his coat and hung it on the stand. Hat too.
He'd not be leaving again in a hurry; he could see through the
window the snow drawing crazy patterns in the air. The streets
would be thickly carpeted soon. He removed his shoes, and
headed for the bedroom. Cheese was on his mind. That smell
of cheese, already occupying the entire flat. In his bedroom he

sat and, before putting his slippers on, cradled each foot for a while. Even through his socks he could feel the miles these extremities had carried him; travels carved into skin which didn't even feel like skin any more; felt like a thick plastic covering, onto which various lumps and ridges had been moulded. The body's journey, written on itself. He planted both feet on the floor and stood, and felt again that wash of dizziness he'd suffered at the foot of the stairs. Careful, Solomon. He reached out for support, and found the handle of the wardrobe door: that was better. Thumping heart, the smell of cheese. A shiver down his back. He should put something warm on, make some tea. There was a cardigan in the wardrobe, so he opened the door and a shape loomed out, sudden and dangerous. Something burst inside old Solomon, though the shape was only briefly there; it had gone, stepped past him, was through the door before Solomon had finished his journey. This had started many years before, very far away, and ended where the floor began. For a moment or two he lingered on the threshold of himself, but the possibility of rejoining his loved ones proved too beguiling to resist, so Solly stepped across whatever the boundary was, and closed the world behind him.

It was much later that Alec Wicinski checked his laptop for search results: he'd become caught up in several matters, each more urgent than a name-chase for an acquaintance. He wanted to get home: travel was going to be a bitch, with tube lines down because of the snow (why? Why did snow affect the underground?) and while he never minded walking, he didn't have shoes for the weather. He texted Sara, confirming their dinner date, filled out his time sheets, then called up the search engines he'd set in motion and scanned the hits: six Peter Kahlmanns, the length and breadth of Europe. Which didn't mean there weren't more, and—allowing for fake IDs—didn't mean there weren't fewer, but it did mean there were six that fell within the parameters of the chosen engines. And this wouldn't have been more than a passing observation were it not for something that rang a bad bell: loud and bastard clear.

One of the Peter Kahlmanns was flagged.

Flagging could have meant any number of things. It could have meant Peter Kahlmann was a friendly, an asset, a joe even; could have meant he was on a watch-list; could have meant he had diplomatic status, and was to be immediately released if he turned up under a hooker's bed during a raid. But what it most definitely meant was, Alec would need a cast-iron reason for having looked him up in the first place. Running a search on a flagged target was like stepping on a tripwire: hard to tell whether you'd done any damage until you lifted your foot again. Everything might be okay, and the world go on as normal. Or you might find your leg blown to kingdom come. Life was full of surprises.

What was certain was that his favour for John Bachelor wasn't a secret any more. When you ran up a flag, someone in the Park saluted.

He cursed under his breath, then closed all the engines

down, not even bothering to examine the particular Peter Kahlmann who'd taken the starring role in his extracurricular trawl. Some things it was better not to know. The bright side was that if Alec had stepped into anything especially messy, he'd not be finding out about it now; he'd have been hauled away and given the treatment the minute he'd fed the name into the system. So with any luck it was a procedural mis-step, no more; one he'd answer for to Richard Pynne, his unlovable shift-manager, come their end of the week catch-up, but not one that had capsized an op. He hoped to God not, anyway. Nothing to do now but cross fingers and hope.

As for Bachelor, he could go whistle. There were favours you did for friends, and there were risks you took for family: Bachelor wasn't the latter and barely qualified as the former. The best Bachelor could hope for was that Alec didn't come looking for him. To point out the error of his ways.

He sighed, powered down and left. Outside, the snow was coming thick and hard: London didn't usually get like this, but when it did, it didn't mess about. It took him two hours to get home, and he missed his date with Sara by a mile. Worse things could happen. Still, that sense of history that Alec carried with him was flickering like a faulty lamp; reminding him that if you expected everything to go tits up, you'd rarely go far wrong.

He'd been woken late evening by a pounding on the door, and a sickening awareness that the Dogs had tracked him down. The pass the dragon at the gate had allowed him had expired hours ago. The place might be in lockdown by now, every corner turned inside out in the hunt for an irregular; a part-time milkman outstaying his welcome.

But you know what, John? That was the best sleep I've had in weeks. As he clambered out of bed, pulled his trousers on, opened the door, Bachelor felt, if not entirely refreshed, at least no worse than when he'd lain down, which was a significant improvement on recent events.

The Dog in question was called Welles, and was new to Bachelor. Time was, he'd kept up with the ground staff at the Park, for the sensible reason that you never knew when you might need a favour, but that was a big ask when you were part-time, and unwelcome on the premises.

"Man, you're in trouble."

"Yeah, yeah. I've been there before."

Except this time, it didn't seem such hostile territory. Welles, after delivering the requisite bollocking, gave him a pitying look and said, "What happened, your wife kick you out?"

As it happened, yes. A while back, but as it could reasonably be seen as the starting pistol on his current circumstances, Bachelor did his best to look sheepish and nod.

"It's a skeleton crew tonight. London's at a standstill because of the snow, and most were let go early. If anyone needs the bed, I'll be back to kick you out. But for now, get your head down. I'll clear it at the desk."

"Thanks. I appreciate that."

"Just don't do it again."

So he climbed out of his trousers once more, and back into

bed, and slept another eight hours, after which he really did feel like a new man; a man who wasn't afraid of what the day might hold. Riding his luck, he showered again, then went to the library and drank two cups of free coffee before leaving the building. The guardian of the gate, a new one, barely batted an eye as he turned in his pass. And then he was out in the world again, and it was a winter wonderland.

It always felt like that, first sight. Pour a couple of tons of snow onto the city streets, and that was all you could see: clean white brightness, all of London's sins forgiven, but it didn't take long for reality to seep through. There wasn't much traffic, but what there was had ploughed the snow, pushing oily puddles of slush into the gutters, and the pavements were punctuated with yellow patches and small piles of filth where London's dogs had relieved themselves. By nightfall, once everything had iced over, romance would have given way to treachery, and every step you took, you'd be worried you'd end up flat on your back. But it was nice to have your philosophy borne out by the facts, thought John Bachelor, as he stood on a snowbound pavement and wondered what to do with his day.

His car was in a long-term near King's Cross, his suitcase in its boot, and this was as much of an address as he currently boasted. But an epic sleep and two showers had set him up well, even if his circumstances had witnessed no improvement overnight. He checked his phone for messages—to see if Alec, Lech, had got back to him—but he was all out of charge. Even that didn't depress him unduly. The snow had provided a time out; nothing would happen for the next little while, which provided him with an alibi of sorts. He could make his way to Solomon's, cadge some breakfast, tell him everything was in hand; that meanwhile, the snow made it impossible for him to get home to Potters Bar, and would it be possible to kip on his sofa? It was a soft way in. He wouldn't have to confess the car crash his life had become. Tomorrow, things would either look different again, or they wouldn't. Either way, he'd have had twenty-four hours to think things over, and at Solly's he was sure of a constant supply of coffee, maybe a good red wine towards the close of play.

So he walked. There were others on the streets, of course, some finding pleasure in the new white world; others plodding grimly through it as if looking forward to the next. On Edgware Road a car had crumpled into a lamp post, attracting an audience, and further along a snowball fight had broken out, apparently good-humoured, but it was early yet. When he reached Solomon's Bachelor rang the bell, but got no answer. He'd grown cold; his overcoat, too thin yesterday, definitely wasn't up to the mark today. He could hang around waiting for Solly to return, or see if he could get a neighbour to buzz him in. This dilemma didn't occupy him long, and on the third time of trying he was inside the building; soon after that, was on bended knee outside Solomon's door, retrieving the spare key. So far so good. He let himself in, called out but got no answer, so went to the kitchen to put the kettle on. Solomon wouldn't mind. Solomon had European manners. There was a stoppered bottle of red on the counter, and Solly wouldn't mind this either, Bachelor decided, pouring a quick glass. It wrapped itself around him like a shroud. He missed this: having a kitchen, having things in it, helping himself to them when he desired. The kettle boiled and switched itself off. Before seeing to it Bachelor removed his coat and went to hang it up, which was when he noticed Solly's bedroom door hanging open. His heart sank. Doors, in Solomon's world, were kept closed. He took a step towards it, then changed his mind; returned to the kitchen, where he poured another, larger glass of wine. He drank it, soaking in the peace and quiet; the muffled quality of the snowed-on city. And then he went to discover the body of his friend.

No drops this time. No clever footwork. He needed to talk to Hannah, in person; no coded messages, no dead-letter she-nanigans. All the fun and games of running an op on foreign soil: Martin had enjoyed teaching Hannah the old ways, but everything had become less funny once the old man dropped dead in front of him. He hadn't meant to scare the bastard; had meant to be long gone before he arrived home, but you couldn't plan for the cosmic fuck-up, and nobody expected to find himself hiding in a wardrobe. He'd left the flat as invisibly as he could, taping the spare key under the mat; had vanished into a whitening world which erased his foot-steps behind him. And had kept both ears on the news ever since, and both eyes on the internet. But nothing yet about a body in a flat off Edgware Road. Which meant either that the body hadn't been found, or that it had been found and was being dangled from a tree in a clearing, while hunters waited in the undergrowth.

So he met Hannah at Liverpool Street Station the following morning, in the bookshop, browsing the thriller section. No surreptitious chat, just a surprised "Gosh, fancy you being here," then a wander into the crowd, thinner than usual because of the snow. The floor was slick with dirty footprints, and the tannoy's announcements were mostly of cancelled trains.

"It's best you don't know why I'm asking," Martin said, "but have any wires been tripped?"

"Something odd happened."

"Tell me."

She told him: Dick the Prick had mentioned his name, on the phone, the previous evening. "Is there any reason why someone would be running a search on your handler?"

"You're my handler, Richard. Is this line secure, by the way?"

"It's fine. And yeah, sure, I'm your . . . handler, but I meant the other one, you know? The one you're only pretending to . . ."

"Pretending to report to."

"Yeah."

"No reason I can think of," she'd told him. "Why?"

She'd asked the question, though the answer was obvious: because someone had done precisely that. Run a search.

Peter Kahlmann was harmless, as far as the Park was concerned; a mediocrity the BND were using to run Hannah, their unimportant mole in an unexciting branch of the British Civil Service. And Peter Kahlmann would carry a little weight if leaned on; Peter Kahlmann wouldn't break at the first hint of pressure. But Peter Kahlmann wasn't indestructible, and if the Park chose to test his strength, he'd splinter and crack eventually, and there—peeping out from the broken shell—would be Martin Kreutzmer, and Martin Kreutzmer was a much more interesting character than Peter Kahlmann. For a start, Martin Kreutzmer wouldn't be running an unimportant mole like Hannah Weiss, which meant that the Park's double agent might require a little more attention herself.

Richard Pynne had said, "So he hasn't said or done anything funny lately? He doesn't suspect that you're not what you claim to be?"

Every triple has moments like this: when they have to consider, for a moment, who and what they claim to be. It largely depends on who they're talking to at the time.

But Hannah had just said, "Nothing's changed. It's not like he's a big deal or anything. I think he regards running me as a chore he's been lumbered with."

And now, in Liverpool Street, Martin said to her: "Good. That's good."

It wasn't good, but you never tell a joe the ground just got swampy.

He asked her to talk while he thought, and she launched into a work anecdote while they paced the station, stepping round or breaking through the queues forming at coffee stands. She was good at this, he registered, even as his mind chewed over other fodder. Whether she'd had this story up her sleeve, whether it had actually happened, whether she was improvising: didn't matter, she delivered it like a natural. And it washed through her while they marched, providing cover for his pondering.

Martin hadn't wanted the old man to die, but these things happened. And if Solomon Dortmund hadn't died then, he'd have died at the first opportunity; the next time a shock was delivered to his door—a backfiring motorbike, a peal of thunder, a telephone, a doorbell. So what mattered now was whether anything could put Martin on the scene. Because he'd thought himself bulletproof, here in bumbling old Blighty, but if the Park got wind that a BND operative had been present when a Service asset died, there'd be retribution. How harsh this might be he wouldn't want to guess, nor would he want to be there when guessing became unnecessary.

And Hannah needed to be secured too. His own position might be in jeopardy, but Hannah's safety was paramount—the joe always came first.

He said, "How far would Pynne stick his neck out for you?"

"Richard? Pretty far, I think."

"And if that wasn't far enough?"

Hannah thought about it, surveying the morose crowds of winter travellers. "I could get him to stick it out further."

"Let's hope it doesn't come to that. But do what you have to."

"What do you need?"

"Find out who ran the search on Peter Kahlmann."

She hugged him, made a loud goodbye; turned to wave when she was ten yards off, and he stood there watching her go: an uncle, a family friend, an innocent colleague, with a rolled-up newspaper under his arm.

The ground was swampy, but once he had the name of whoever had been checking his cover story out, he'd know what to do. If it had rung Pynne's bells, it must have come from within Regent's Park, but Pynne himself obviously didn't know why it had happened. Which might mean it had come from up the ladder, above Pynne's head, which probably meant game over: that Martin and Hannah would have to up sticks. But if it was someone lower down—someone who'd wandered off reservation on their lonesome—well. There might be other ways of solving the problem. Martin was old school, and rarely indulged in dirty work, but there were others within reach, a phone call away, who had different skills, different talents. They could turn a man's life upside down without laying a finger on him. If that happened to you, you'd quickly forget whatever extracurricular games you'd been playing. You'd be too busy trying to plug the leaks you'd sprung, and hoping the damage wasn't permanent.

He left Liverpool Street, noting that the sky overhead was still a grey vault, and the air still bit back when you breathed it. There'd be more of this weather before there was less. He wasn't entirely sure the English language would bear that construction, but it sounded right in his head, and there was no one around to correct him.

John Bachelor sat for a while, drinking the wine, deciding he might as well eat. Solomon had been shopping; there were bags of food in the kitchen, still awaiting unpacking. Fresh bread, cheese;

chocolately treats. Tins of sardines. There was no point letting it go to waste. And nothing he could do right now about reporting Solly's death: his phone was still uncharged, and his charger was in his car. There was a department to ring in these circumstances, and a telephone in the flat, but Bachelor didn't know the number by heart, couldn't read it on his powerless phone, and tracking it down would mean talking to half a dozen suspicious civil servants. No, he'd sit a while before putting it all in motion: the necessary investigation, the endless reports, the winding down of Solomon's afterlife—his Service pension, his flat.

He went to take another look at the body. There were no signs of violence, and it was clear from the shopping that Solly had not been in the flat long when he died. Bachelor, not a doctor, reached the obvious conclusion: Solly had over-exerted himself doing an emergency shop, and this was the result. It was sad but it must have been quick, and among other things meant that Bachelor no longer felt obliged to indulge Solomon's final whimsy. The drop, the *pas de deux* Solomon thought he'd seen in Fischer's, had been nothing more than an ancient asset's final glimpse down the twists of Spook Street. Even if Bachelor put it on file, there'd be no follow-up; it would be dismissed as an old man's fantasy. Alec, if he'd run Kahlmann's name through the databases yet, had done so as a favour to Bachelor; he wasn't putting it through channels. So the drop could be quietly dropped, which meant that Solomon's passing would cause no more a ruffle than a passing pigeon. All Bachelor needed to do was write up today's one-sided visit, sign his name, and attend the funeral.

A stray thought wafted past, and whispered in his ear.

He dismissed it and made a cheese sandwich; ate looking down from Solomon's window to the muffled street below. It was warm inside; heating was paid by direct debit, from a Service account, and as this had been set up in the days before austerity—when people were valued for what they had done, rather than dismissed out of hand for being no longer capable of doing it—it was a generous monthly sum, ensuring Solomon need never grow cold. Like everything else to do with Bachelor's charges, the process was automatic and unquestioned. That was one thing about the Civil Service: once it decided to do something, it carried on doing it. It would march on, indestructible, and sooner or later would probably inherit the earth, though when it did, it wouldn't do anything with it that it hadn't already been doing for centuries.

His sandwich eaten, Bachelor remained where he was, mulling options. As usual, there weren't many available. But for now, at least—warm and comfortable—he was in no hurry to exercise choice; he'd just sit for a bit and watch the snow. In the other room lay Solomon Dortmund, but that was okay. The old man had learned patience in life, and there was no reason why this virtue should abandon him now.

The snow lingered for days, hardening to ice on the pavements, the better to keep a grip, and though traffic reasserted itself eventually, it did so with a chastened air, reminded of its place in the great chain of being: the car was king of the road, but only while the weather allowed. Shops that had been closed opened up, and opportunist roadside vending vans moved on. In Regent's Park, the hub had maintained its quiet buzz throughout the hiatus, but the surrounding offices were only just coming back to life, proving what Alec Wicinski and his colleagues had long known: that actual work continues untroubled, regardless of management's presence. As for Alec himself, he hadn't turned up that morning, causing troubled glances among the boys and girls of the hub. Unexplained absence was a cause of concern in their world.

In her office, Lady Di was grilling Richard Pynne.

"When did it come to light?"

"During yesterday evening's sweep."

"And there'd been no previous hint of . . . anything?"

Pynne shook his head.

He hadn't been at the Park lately, frozen lines having made his commute near-impossible, but he'd bravely struggled into town to meet Snow White the evening before last. He'd worried when he got her call, an emergency-only code, and had spent the expensive cab ride picturing any manner of calamity. In his imagination, she was being hauled into a cellar by disgruntled BND operatives. So to find her fine—perky, even—was more than a relief; it was cause for celebration.

"I'm sorry, Richard. I got a case of the frights. But I'm okay now."

"It happens." Their hug went on longer than he'd expected. "Joes in the field, you're allowed to get the frights. That's what I'm here for. To make them go away again."

Instead of coffee and a chocolate, they'd snuggled down in a bar off Wardour Street, and at her suggestion he'd ordered tequila slammers. Just the thing to chase the jitters away. And a legitimate expense, almost certainly.

Inevitably, things had become hazy towards the end. She'd asked, he remembered, about what he'd said the previous day; those mysterious questions concerning Peter Kahlmann, and he'd explained, fuzzily, that he couldn't go into details; that a flag had been raised because someone on the hub had run a search on Kahlmann, and no, he couldn't tell her who. Clashified information. She'd laughed: You sound like James Bond. *On Her Majeshty's Shecret Shervish*. He'd laughed too: I preferred Roger Moore. It had been a crazy evening. Crazy. But he was almost certain he'd not mentioned Alec Wicinski by name. Which would have meant nothing to Hannah anyway.

So yesterday he'd stayed off work using snow as an excuse, but the truth was he'd got home so loaded, he'd barely been able to crawl out of bed in the morning. His first few hours had been spent cradled over the toilet. Touch of flu, he'd phoned in: yeah yeah yeah. And then, come evening, when he was just about upright again, the results of the weekly remote sweep of the boys' and girls' laptops came in.

Which is when the problem with Wicinski came to light.

Pynne said, "The laptop's been in Alec's sole possession. The download took place outside office hours, but that's neither here nor . . . Thing is, he's claiming not to know anything about it, but he would, wouldn't he? And if anyone else gained access to his machine, that in itself's a disciplinary offence. These things are beyond classified. That's the first thing they tell you when you're given one."

This hadn't prevented their being left in cabs or on trains, but that wasn't the issue right now.

Di Taverner said, "And the download's illegal?"

"Child porn," said Pynne. "It's . . . they're saying it's pretty disgusting."

"Yes, the clue's in the name." She glanced towards the hub, and half a dozen faces turned quickly away. Sighing, she reached for the switch that frosted her glass wall. "Could it have been planted remotely?"

"IT says yes, technically, but it would require serious, state of the art intervention. Another Service might have the where-withal to hack into one of our laptops and dump that stuff there from a distance, but it's not something a kid's done in his bedroom. And that being so, why would they? Why would another Service want to frame Wicinski?"

"What's he working on?"

"Nothing to put anyone's back up."

"You're sure?"

Pynne was sure, or at least, he was sure that was the answer he wanted to give. Coincidences happened, everyone knew that. Had he mentioned Alec's name to Snow White? He was pretty certain not. Besides, Alec was on his team, his name cropped up all the time. Alec this and Alec that. That was the nature of being a manager: your team was always on your radar.

"Where is he now?"

"Dogs."

Through the frosted wall came the dim suggestion of movement. That would also be the Dogs, here to ransack Lech Wicinski's workstation and dismantle his hardware. His locker would have been turned out by now too. Either more evidence of his moral corruption would be found, or he'd be shown to have buried it completely—this slip-up aside, that is.

"I can believe he gets off on that stuff," she said. "Everyone has a dark side. What I don't understand is why he'd download it onto our laptop."

Pynne didn't know either. But he said, "If you get away with something for long enough, you start to think you're too clever to be caught."

"So he's been doing it for a while?"

There were any number of pitfalls here, chief among them that he'd be called to account for not having rumbled Wicinski's predilections earlier. "There've been no indications of aberrant behaviour. He's always passed the psych tests. But . . ."

"But if it wasn't possible to disguise the urge, we'd all know who the paedophiles were," she finished. "Jesus, Richard."

It crossed his mind to offer comfort, but he wisely kept his mouth shut.

She said, "He'll have to go on suspension. While the Dogs do whatever they need to do."

Pynne said, "It's a criminal offence. Shouldn't we pass it to the Met?"

"And enjoy another season of spook-bashing? I don't think so. Things are bad enough without gifting the tabloids their headlines. No, we'll handle this in-house. If he's got any sense, he'll come clean without letting the whole thing drag on too long." She defrosted the window. "And then it'll be just how we like it. Everything out in the open."

He could rarely tell, with Lady Di, where the irony stopped.

She shifted gear. "How's Snow White coming along?"

"Fine," he said. "Her transfer's come through. She starts in the Brexit office Monday."

"And it's all going smoothly? The two of you?"

"Yes."

"Good. It's not an easy business, running an agent. Even on friendly soil. If this continues to go well, we'll think about expanding your brief. But I'll need to be sure you're up to it."

"Thank you." He stood to go, but paused at the door. "What'll happen to him? Alec?"

"If he turns out guilty?"

He nodded.

She said, "Well, we can't sack him. Not without inviting attendant publicity. But he can't stay here, obviously. Not that he'd want to, now his secret's out in the open." She reached for her laptop, tapped in her password. "Just as well we've somewhere we can put him."

"Oh," said Pynne.

"Yes," said Diana Taverner. "Man's got a nasty kink. Slough House should be right up his street."

And the snow stays where it is, and the weather doesn't turn, and the streets remain cold, and the days are dark from dawn to dusk. In different parts of London, different people feel different things. Alec Wicinski is mostly numb, dumbfounded by the speed with which his life has spiralled into hell, while Martin Kreutzmer has the sense of having narrowly avoided disaster, and can now see a clear path ahead, leading steadily upwards. Hannah has started in her new role, where it is apparent she will have access to information useful to the folk back home; together, the pair look set to enjoy many a triumph. And it's a pleasure to hoodwink another Service, especially when that Service thinks it's hoodwinking you. Contemplating the last few days, Martin gives silent thanks to the BND's sneaker team, who can walk through the Park's firewalls, and leave packages in laptops the way couriers leave parcels in dustbins—without notice, and undetected—but if he spares a thought for the poor bastard on the receiving end, it's a brief one. Martin has been playing this game a long time, and knows that, like those of politicians, all spies' lives end in failure. The best among them fade away with no one having suspected their true calling; for others, the end comes sooner, and that is all. It is part of the game. He lights a rare cigar and wonders what his next move will be. There's no hurry. The game lasts forever.

As for John Bachelor, he spends a lot of time at Solomon's window, looking down on what once were Solomon's streets. Solomon himself has been taken away, of course. An ambulance removed the body; a police officer came and took notes. Bachelor faked nothing, just described what had happened: he'd arrived to check on the old man, and the old man didn't

come to the door. There was a spare key taped under the mat
. . . His cover held up. There is an actual company, existing
on paper, by which he is employed to visit the elderly and
infirm, ensuring their needs are catered for, their lives secure
and intact; the sort of service once provided free by society,
before the 1980s happened. There'll be a funeral next week.
He's called the numbers in Solomon's address book, kept by
the phone. He's booked a room in a pub, and will put money
behind the bar.

But he hasn't informed the Park. That stray thought that
wafted past him, the same hour he found Solomon's body,
returned, and returned again, and somehow clarified into
intention. He has not informed Regent's Park that Solomon
Dortmund is dead. So Solomon's pension will continue to be
paid, and Solomon's flat will continue to be warm. It will only
be for a short while, he tells himself; just until he has found
his feet again, and it's not precisely corruption—is it?—more
administrative streamlining. He's a free-floating irregular,
poorly paid and unsupervised; if he chooses to keep his
reports free of burdensome detail, that is up to him. It's not
like anyone else is keeping an eye on his milk round. And he
will do his job better, be more alert to his charges' needs, if
he isn't worrying about his own life circumstances; if he has
somewhere to lay his head at night.

It occurs to him that he never heard back from Alec
Wicinski, but that's a detail that has ceased to matter, and it
won't bother him long.

And meanwhile the streetlights come on, and the view

from the window thickens and slows. He remains where he is for a while, fascinated by the world he is no longer locked out in. There are no guarantees, he knows; his stratagem could be discovered at any time, and then he'll be for the high jump. Right now, though, John Bachelor is warm, he is fed; there is wine in Solomon's larder. In a minute, he'll go pour himself a glass. But for now he'll sit and watch the quiet snow.

Continue reading for a preview of

LONDON RULES

The killers arrived in a sand-coloured jeep, and made short work of the village.

There were five of them and they wore mismatched military gear, two opting for black and the others for piebald variations. Neckerchiefs covered the lower half of their faces, sunglasses the upper, and their feet were encased in heavy boots, as if they'd crossed the surrounding hills the hard way. From their belts hung sundry items of battleground kit. As the first emerged from the vehicle he tossed a water bottle onto the seat behind him, an action replicated in miniature in his aviator lenses.

It was approaching noon, and the sun was as white as the locals had known it. Somewhere nearby, water tumbled over stones. The last time trouble had called here, it had come bearing swords.

Out of the car, by the side of the road, the men stretched and spat. They didn't talk. They seemed in no hurry, but at the same time were focused on what they were doing. This was part of the operation: arrive, limber up, regain flexibility. They had driven a long way in the heat. No sense starting before they were in tune with their limbs and could trust their reflexes. It didn't matter that they were attracting attention, because nobody watching could alter what was to happen. Forewarned would not mean forearmed. All the villagers had were sticks.

One of these—an ancient thing bearing many of the characteristics of its parent tree, being knobbled and imprecise, sturdy and reliable—was leaned on by an elderly man whose weathered looks declared him farming stock. But somewhere in his history, perhaps, lurked a memory of war, for of all those watching the visitors perform their callisthenics he alone seemed to understand their intent, and into his eyes, already a little tearful from the sunshine, came both fear and a kind of resignation, as if he had always known that this, or something like it, would rear up and swallow him. Not far away, two women broke off from conversation. One held a cloth bag. The other's hands moved slowly towards her mouth. A barefoot boy wandered through a doorway into sunlight, his features crumpling in the glare.

In the near distance a chain rattled as a dog tested its limits. Inside a makeshift coop, its mesh and wooden struts a patchwork of recycled materials, a chicken squatted to lay an egg no one would ever collect.

From the back of their jeep the men fetched weapons, sleek and black and awful.

The last ordinary noise was the one the old man made when

he dropped his stick. As he did so his lips moved, but no sound emerged.

And then it began.

From afar, it might have been fireworks. In the surrounding hills birds took to the air in a frightened rattle, while in the village itself cats and dogs leaped for cover. Some bullets went wild, sprayed in indiscriminate loops and skirls, as if in imitation of a local dance; the chicken coop was blasted to splinters, and scars were chipped into stones that had stood unblemished for centuries. But others found their mark. The old man followed his stick to the ground, and the two women were hurled in opposite directions, thrown apart by nodules of lead that weighed less than their fingers. The barefoot boy tried to run. In the hillsides were tunnels carved into rock, and given time he might have found his way there, waited in the darkness until the killers had gone, but this possibility was blasted out of existence by a bullet that caught him in the neck, sending him cartwheeling down the short slope to the river, which was little more than a trickle today. The villagers caught in the open were scattering now, running into the fields, seeking shelter behind walls and in ditches; even those who hadn't seen what was happening had caught the fear, for catastrophe is its own herald, trumpeting its arrival to early birds and stragglers alike. It has a certain smell, a certain pitch. It sends mothers shrieking for their young, the old looking for God.

And two minutes later it was over, and the killers left. The jeep, which had idled throughout the brief carnage, spat stones as it accelerated away, and for a short while there was stillness. The sound of the departing engine folded into the landscape and was lost. A buzzard mewed overhead. Closer to home a gurgle sounded in a ruined throat, as someone struggled with a new language, whose first words were their last. And behind that, and then above it, and soon all around it, grew the screams of the survivors, for whom all familiar life was over, just as it was for the dead.

Within hours trucks would come bearing more men with guns, this time trained outwards, on the surrounding hillsides. Helicopters would land, disgorging doctors and military personnel, and others would fly overhead, crisscrossing the sky in orchestrated rage, while TV cameras pointed and blamed. On the streets shrouds would cover the fallen, and newly loosed chickens would wander by the river, pecking in the dirt. A bell would ring, or at least, people would remember it ringing. It might have been in their minds. But what was certain was that there would still be, above the buzzing helicopters, a sky whose blue remained somehow unbroken, and a distant buzzard mewing, and long shadows cast by the stunned Derbyshire hills.

In some parts of the world dawn arrives with rosy fingers, to smoothe away the creases left by night. But on Aldersgate Street, in the London borough of Finsbury, it comes wearing safecracker's gloves, so as not to leave prints on windowsills and doorknobs; it squints through keyholes, sizes up locks and generally cases the joint ahead of approaching day. Dawn specialises in unswept corners and undusted surfaces, in the nooks and chambers day rarely sees, because day is all business appointments and things being in the right place, while its younger sister's role is to creep about in the breaking gloom, never sure of what it might find there. It's one thing casting light on a subject. It's another expecting it to shine.

So when dawn reaches Slough House—a scruffy building whose ground floor is divided between an ailing Chinese restaurant and a desperate newsagent's, and whose front door, made filthy by time and weather, never opens—it enters by the burglar's route, via the rooftops opposite, and its first port of call is Jackson Lamb's office, this being on the uppermost

storey. Here it finds its only working rival a standard lamp atop
a pile of telephone directories, which have so long served this
purpose they have moulded together, their damp covers bond-
ing in involuntary alliance. The room is cramped and furtive,
like a kennel, and its overpowering theme is neglect. Psycho-
paths are said to decorate their walls with crazy writing, the
loops and whorls of their infinite equations an attempt at
cracking the code their life is hostage to. Lamb prefers his walls
to do their own talking, and they have cooperated to the extent
that the cracks in their plasterwork, their mildew stains, have
here and there conspired to produce something that might
amount to an actual script—a scrawled observation, perhaps—
but all too quickly any sense these marks contain blurs and
fades, as if they were something a moving finger had writ before
deciding, contrary to the wisdom of ages, to rub out again.

Lamb's is not a room to linger in, and dawn, anyway, never
tarries long. In the office opposite, it finds less to disturb it.
Here order has prevailed, and there is a quiet efficiency about
the way in which folders have been stacked, their edges squared
off in alignment with the desktop, and the ribbons binding
them tied in bows of equal length; about the emptiness of the
wastepaper basket, and the dust-free surfaces of the well-man-
nered shelves. There is a stillness here out of keeping with
Slough House, and if one were to seesaw between these two
rooms, the bossman's lair and Catherine Standish's bolt-hole,
a balance might be found that could bring peace to the premises, though one would imagine it would be short-lived.

As is dawn's presence in Catherine's room, for time is

hurrying on. On the next level down is a kitchen. Dawn's favourite meal is breakfast, which is sometimes mostly gin, but either way it would find little to sustain it here, the cupboards falling very much on Scrooge's end of the Dickensian curve, far removed from Pickwickian excess. The cupboards contain no tins of biscuits, no jars of preserves, no emergency chocolate and no bowls of fruit or packets of crispbread mar the counter's surface; just odds and ends of plastic cutlery, a few chipped mugs and a surprisingly new-looking kettle. True, there is a fridge, but all it holds are two cans of energy drink, both stickered "Roddy Ho," each of which rubric has had the words "is a twat" added, in different hands, and an uncontested tub of hummus, which is either mint-flavoured or has some other reason for being green. About the appliance hangs an odour best described as delayed decay. Luckily, dawn has no sense of smell.

Having briefly swept through the two offices on this floor—nondescript rooms whose colour schemes can only be found in ancient swatches, their pages so faded, everything has subsided into shades of yellow and grey—and taken care to skirt the dark patch beneath the radiator, where some manner of rusty leakage has occurred, it finds itself back on the staircase, which is old and rackety, dawn the only thing capable of using it without making a sound—apart, that is, from Jackson Lamb, who when he feels like it can wander Slough House as silently as a newly conjured wraith, if rather more corpulent. At other times Lamb prefers the direct approach, and attacks the stairs with the noise that a bear pushing a wheelbarrow might make, if the wheelbarrow was full of tin cans, and the bear drunk.

More watchful ghost than drunken bear, dawn arrives in the final two offices and finds little to distinguish them from those on the floor above, apart, perhaps, from the slightly stuccoed texture of the paintwork behind one desk, as if a fresh coat has been applied before the wall has been properly cleaned, and some lumpy matter has been left clinging to the plasterwork: best not to dwell on what this might be. For the rest, this office has the same air of frustrated ambition as its companions, and to one as sensitive as light-fingered dawn it contains, too, a memory of violence, and perhaps the promise of more to come. But dawn understands that promises are easily broken—dawn knows all about breaking—and the possibility delays it not one jot. On it goes, down the final set of stairs, and somehow passes through the back door without recourse to the shove this usually requires, the door being famously resistant to casual use. In the dank little yard behind Slough House dawn pauses, aware that its time is nearly up, and enjoys these last cool moments. Once upon a time it might have heard a horse making its way up the street; more recently, the happy hum of a milk float would have whiled away its final minute. But today there is only the scream of an ambulance, late for an appointment, and by the time its banshee howl has ceased bouncing off walls and buildings dawn has disappeared, and here in its place is the day itself, which, once within Slough House's grasp, turns out to be far from the embodiment of industry and occupation it threatened to be. Instead—like the day before it, and the one before that— it is just another slothful interlude to be clock watched out of existence, and knowing full well that none of the inhabitants can do anything to hasten its departure, it takes its own sweet time about setting up shop. Casually, smugly, unbothered by doubt or duty, it divides itself between Slough House's offices, and then, like a lazy cat, settles in the warmest corners to doze, while nothing much happens around it.

Roddy Ho, Roddy Ho, riding through the glen.

(Just another earworm.)

Roddy Ho, Roddy Ho, manliest of men.

There are those who regard Roderick Ho as a one-trick wonder; a king of the keyboard jungle, sure, but less adept in other areas of life, such as making friends, being reasonable, and ironing T-shirts. But they haven't seen him in action. They haven't seen him on the prowl.

Lunchtime, just off Aldersgate Street. The ugly concrete towers of the Barbican to the right; a hardly more beautiful housing estate to the left. But it's a killing box, this uncelebrated patch of London; it's a blink-and-you're-eaten battlefield. You get one chance only to claim your scalp, and Roddy Ho's prey could be anywhere.

He knew damn well it was close.

So he moved, pantherlike, between parked cars; he hovered by a placard celebrating some municipal triumph or other. In his ear, driven like a fence post by the pounding of his iPod, an overexcited forty-something screeched tenderly of his plan to kill and eat his girlfriend. On Roddy's chin, the beard he'd grown last winter; rather more expertly sculpted now, because he'd learned the hard way not to use kitchen scissors. On Roddy's head—new development—a baseball cap. Image matters, Roddy knew that. *Brand* matters. You want Joe Public to recognise your avatar, your avatar had to make a statement. In his own personal opinion, he'd nailed that angle. Neat little goatee and a baseball cap: originality plus style. Roderick Ho was the complete package, the way Brad Pitt used to be, before the unpleasantness.

(Gap in the market there, come to think of it. He'd have to have a word with Kim, his girlfriend, about coining a *nom de celeb*.

Koddy.

Rim . . . ?

Nah. Needs work.)

But he'd deal with that later, because right now it was time to activate the lure module; get this creature into the open and bring that sucker *down*. This required force, timing and use of weapons: his core skills in a nutshell . . . Whoever came up with *Pokémon GO* must have had Roderick Ho on their muse's speed dial. The name even rhymed, man—it was like he was born to poke. Gimme that stardust, he thought. Gimme that lovely stardust, and watch the Rodster *shine*.

All reflex, sinew and concentration, Ho shimmered through the lunchtime air like the coolest of cats, the baddest of asses, the daddy of all dudes; hot on the trail of an enemy that didn't exist.

A little way down the road, an enemy that did turned the ignition, and pulled away from the kerb.

That morning, on her way to the Tube, Catherine Standish had dropped in at the newsagent's for a *Guardian*. Behind the counter a steel blind had been drawn to hide the array of cigarette packets, lest a stray glimpse prove a gateway to early death, while to her left, on the topmost row of the rack, the few pornographic magazines to survive into the digital age were sealed inside plastic covers, to nullify their impact on concupiscent minds. All this careful protection, she thought, shielding us from impulses deemed harmful, but right there by the door was a shelf of wine on special offer, any two bottles for £9, and up by the counter was a range of spirits all cheerfully marked two quid down, none of them a brand to delight the palate, but any of them enough to render the most uptight connoisseur pig-drunk and open to offers.

She bought her newspaper, nodded her thanks and returned to the street.

One journey later, she remembered it was her turn to pick up milk for the office—no huge feat of memory; it was always her turn to pick up milk—and dropped into the shop next to Slough House, where the milk was in the fridge alongside cans of beer and lager, and ready-mixed tins of G&T. That's twice without trying, she thought, that she could have bought a ticket to the underworld before her day was off the ground. Most occasions of sin required a little effort. But the recovering alcoholic could coast along in neutral, and the temptations would come to her.

There was nothing unusual about this. It was just the surface tension; the everyday gauntlet the dry drunk runs. Come lunchtime, the lure of the dark side behind her, Catherine was absorbed in the day's work: writing up the department's biannual accounts, which included justification for "irregular expenses." Slough House had had a lot of these this year: broken doors, carpet cleaning; all the making-good an armed incursion demands. Most of the repairs had been sloppily done, which neither surprised nor bothered Catherine much: she had long ago grown used to the second-class status the slow horses enjoyed. What worried her more was the long-term damage to the horses themselves. Shirley Dander was unnervingly calm; the kind of calm Catherine imagined icebergs were, just before they ploughed into ocean liners. River Cartwright was bottling things up too, more than usual. And as for J.K. Coe, Catherine recognised a hand grenade when she saw one. And she didn't think his pin was fitted too tight.

Roddy Ho was the same as ever, of course, but that was more of a burden than a comfort.

It was a good job Louisa Guy was relatively sane.

Stacks of paper in front of her, their edges neatly though not quite neurotically aligned, Catherine waded through the day's work, adjusting figures where Lamb's entries overshot the inaccurate to become manifestly corrupt, and replacing his justifications ("because I fucking say so") with her own more diplomatic phrasing. When the time came to leave for home, all those temptations would parade in front of her again. But if daily exposure to Jackson Lamb had taught her anything, it was not to fret about life's peripheral challenges.

He had a way of providing more than enough to worry about, up front and centre.

Shirley Dander had sixty-two days.

Sixty-two drug-free days.

Count 'em . . .

Somebody might: Shirley didn't. Sixty-two was just a number, same as sixty-one had been, and if she happened to be keeping track that was only because the days had all happened in the obvious order, very, very slowly. Mornings she ticked off the minutes, and afternoons counted down seconds, and at least once a day found herself staring at the walls, particularly the one behind what had been Marcus's desk. Last time she'd seen Marcus, he'd been leaning against that wall, his chair tilted at a ridiculous angle. It had been painted over since. A bad job had been made of it.

And here was Shirley's solution to that: think about something else.

It was lunchtime; bright and warm. Shirley was heading back to Slough House for an afternoon of enforced inertia, after which she'd schlep on over to Shoreditch for the last of her AFMs . . . Eight months of anger fucking management sessions, and this evening she'd officially be declared anger free. It had been hinted she might even get a badge. That could be a problem—if anyone stuck a badge on her, they'd be carrying their teeth home in a hankie—but luckily, what she had in her pocket gave her something to focus on; to carry her through any dodgy moments which might result in the court-ordered programme being extended.

A neat little wrap of the best cocaine the postcode had to offer; her treat to herself for finishing the course.

Sixty-two might just be a number, but it was as high as Shirley had any intention of going.

Being straight had had the effect of turning her settings down a notch, and the world had been flatter lately, greyer, easier to get along with. Which helped with the whole AFM thing, but was starting to piss her off. Last week she'd had a cold-caller, some crap about mis-sold insurance, and Shirley hadn't even told him to fuck himself. This didn't feel like attitude adjustment so much as it did surrender. So here was the plan: get through this one last day, suffer being patted on the head by the counsellor—whom Shirley intended to follow home one night and kill—then hit the clubs, get properly wasted and learn to live again. Sixty-two days was long enough, and proved for a fact what she'd always maintained as a theory: that she could give it up any time she wanted.

Besides, Marcus was long gone. It wasn't like he'd be getting in her face about it.

But don't think about Marcus.

So there she was, heading past the estate towards Aldersgate Street, coke in her pocket, mind on the evening to come, when she saw two things five yards in front of her, both behaving strangely.

One was Roderick Ho, who was performing some kind of ballet, with a mobile phone for a partner.

The other was an approaching silver Honda, turning left where there was no left to turn.

Then mounting the pavement and heading straight for Ho.

So here's the thing, thought Louisa Guy. If I'd wanted to be a librarian, I'd have been a librarian. I'd have gone to library school, taken library exams and saved up enough library stamps to buy a library uniform. Whatever they do, I'd have done it: by the book. And of all the librarians in the near vicinity, I'd have been far and away the librarianest; the kind of librarian other librarians sing songs about, gathered around their library fires.

But what I wouldn't have done was join the intelligence service. Because that would have been fucking ridiculous.

Yet here I am.

Here she was.

Here being Slough House, where what she was doing was scrolling through library loan statistics, determining who had borrowed certain titles in the course of the last few years. Books like *Islam Expects* and *The Meaning of Jihad*. And if anyone had actually written *How to Wage War on a Civilian Population*, that would have made the list too.

"Is it really likely," she'd said, on being handed the project, "that compiling a list of people who've borrowed particular library books is going to help us find fledgling terrorists?"

"Put like that," Lamb had said, "the odds are probably a million to one." He shook his head. "I'll tell you this for nothing. I'm bloody glad I'm not you."

"Thanks. But why do they even stock these books, if they're so dangerous?"

"It's political correctness gone mad," agreed Lamb sadly. "I'm rabidly anticensorship, as you know. But some books just need burning."

So did some bosses. She'd been working on this list, which involved cross-checking Public Lending Right statistics against individual county library databases, for three months. It now stretched not quite halfway down a single sheet of A4, and she'd reached Buckinghamshire in her alphabetical list of counties. Thank Christ she didn't have to cover the whole of the UK, because that would have taken even an actual librarian years.

Not the whole of it, no. Just England, Wales and Northern Ireland.

"Fuck Scotland," Lamb had explained. "They want to go it alone, they can go it alone."

Her only ally in her never-ending task was the Government, which was doing its bit by closing down as many libraries as possible.

In the War Against Terror, you take all the help you can get.

Louisa giggled to herself, because sometimes you had to, or else you'd go mad. Unless the giggling was proof you'd already gone mad. J.K. Coe might know, not so much because of his so-called expertise in Psychological Evaluation, but because he was a borderline nutter himself. All fun and games in Slough House.

She pushed away from her desk and stood to stretch. Lately

she'd been spending more time at the gym, and the result was increasing restlessness when tethered to her computer. Through the window, Aldersgate Street was its usual unpromising medley of pissed-off traffic and people in a hurry. Nobody ever wandered through this bit of London; it was just a staging post on the way somewhere else. Unless you were a stalled spook, of course, in which case it was journey's end.

God, she was bored.

And then, as if to console her, the world threw a minor distraction her way: from not far off came a screech and a bump; the sound of a car making contact.

She wondered what that was about.

Hi Tina

Just a quick note to let you know how things are going here in Devon—not great, to be honest. I've been told I'm being laid off at the end of the month because the boss's sister's son needs a job, so someone has to make way for the little bastard. Thanks a bunch, right?

But it's not all bad because the gaffer knows he owes me one, and has set me up with one of his contacts for a six-month gig in—get this—Albania! But it's a cushy number, doing the wiring on three new hotel builds, and it'll be cheap living so I'll

Coe stopped midsentence and stared through the window at the Barbican opposite. It was an Orwellian nightmare of a complex, a concrete monstrosity, but credit where it was due:

like Ronnie and Reggie Kray before it, the Barbican had over-
come the drawback of being a brutal piece of shit to achieve
iconic status. But that was London Rules for you: force others
to take you on your own terms. And if they didn't like it, stay
in their face until they did.

Jackson Lamb, for instance. Except, on second thoughts, no:
Lamb didn't give a toss whose terms you took him on. He
carried on regardless. He just *was*.

Tina, though, wasn't, or wouldn't be much longer. Tina
wasn't her real name anyway. J.K. Coe just found it easier to
compose these letters if they had an actual name attached; for
the same reason, he always signed them Dan. Dan—whoever
he was—was a deep cover spook, who'd moled into whichever
group of activists was currently deemed too extreme for comfort (animal rights, eco-troublemakers, *The Archers*' fanbase);
while Tina—whoever *she* was—was someone he'd befriended
in the course of doing so. There was always a Tina. Back when
Coe had been in Psych Eval, he'd made a study of Tinas of
both genders; joes in the field were warned not to develop
emotional attachments in the group under investigation, but
they always did. You couldn't betray someone efficiently if you
didn't love them first. So when the op was over, and Dan was
coming back to the surface, there had to be letters; a long
goodbye played out over months. First Dan moved out of the
area, a fair distance off but not unvisitable. He'd keep in touch
sporadically, then get a better offer and move abroad. The
letters or emails would falter, then stop. And soon Dan would
be forgotten, by everyone but Tina, who'd keep his letters in a

shoebox under her bed, and Google-Earth Albania after her third glass of Chardonnay. Rather than, for example, dragging him into court for screwing her under false pretences. Nobody wanted to go through that again.

But of course, joes don't write the letters themselves. That was a job for spooks like J.K. Coe, whiling away the days in Slough House. And lucky to be doing so, to be honest. Most people who'd shot to death a handcuffed man might have expected retribution. Luckily, Coe had done so at the fag-end of a series of events so painfully compromising to the intelligence services as a whole that—as Lamb had observed—it had put the "us" in "clusterfuck," leaving Regent's Park with little choice but to lay a huge carpet over everything and sweep Slough House under it. The slow horses were used to that, of course. In fact, if they weren't already slow horses, they'd be dust bunnies instead.

Coe cracked his knuckles, and added the words *be able to save a bit* to his letter. Yeah, right; Dan would save a bit, then meet an Albanian girl, and—long story short—never come home. Meanwhile, the actual Dan would be undercover again, on a different op, and the ball would be rolling in a new direction. On Spook Street, things never stayed still. Unless you were in Slough House, that is. But there was a major difference between J.K. Coe and the other slow horses, and it was this: he had no desire to be where the action was. If he could sit here typing all day and never have to say a word to anyone, that would suit him fine. Because his life was approaching an even keel. The dreams were ebbing away at last, and the panic attacks had tapered off. He no longer found himself obsessively fingering an imaginary keyboard, echoing Keith Jarrett's improvised piano solos. Things were bearable, and might just stay that way provided nothing happened.

He hoped like hell nothing would happen.

The car smeared Roderick Ho like ketchup across the concrete apron; broke him like a plastic doll across its bonnet, so all that was holding him together was his clothes. This happened so fast Shirley saw it before it took place. Which was as well for Ho, because she had time to prevent it.

She covered five yards with the speed of a greased pig, yelling Ho's name, though he didn't turn round—he had his back to the car and his iPod jammed into his ears; was squinting through his smartphone, and looked, basically, like a dumb tourist who'd been ripped off twice already: once by someone selling hats, and a second time by someone giving away beards. When Shirley hit him waist-high, he was apparently taking a photo of bugger-all. But he never got the chance. Shirley's weight sent him crashing to the ground half a moment before the car ploughed past: went careering across the pedestrianised area, bounced off a low brick wall bordering a garden display then screeched to a halt. Burnt rubber reached Shirley's nose. Ho was squawking; his phone was in pieces. The car moved again, but instead of heading back for them it circled the brick enclosure, turned left onto the road, swerved round the barrier and went east.

Shirley watched it disappear, too late to catch its plate, or even clock the number of occupants. Soon she'd feel the impact of her leap in most of her bones, but for the moment she just replayed it in her head from a third-party viewpoint: a graceful, gazelle-like swoop; lifesaving moment and poetry in motion at once. Marcus would have been proud, she thought.

Dead proud.

Beneath her, Roddy yelled, "You stupid cow!"

The internet was full of whispers.

No, River Cartwright thought. Scratch that.

The internet was screaming its head off, as usual.

He was on a Marylebone-bound train, returning to London after having taken the morning off: care leave, he'd claimed it, though Lamb preferred "bloody liberty."

"We're not the social services."

"We're not Sports Direct either," Catherine Standish had pointed out. "If River needs the morning off, he needs it."

"And who's gunna pick up his workload in the meantime?"

River hadn't done a stroke of work in three weeks, but didn't think this a viable line of defence. "It'll get done," he promised.

And Lamb had grunted, and that was that.

So he'd taken off in the pre-breakfast rush, battling against the commuter tide; heading for Skylarks, the care home where the O.B. now resided; not precisely a Service-run facility—the Service had long since outsourced any such frivolities—but one which placed a higher priority on security than most places of its type.

The Old Bastard, River's grandfather, had wandered off down the twilit corridors of his own mind, only occasionally emerging into the here and now, whereupon he'd sniff the air like an elderly badger and look pained, though whether this was due to a brief awareness that his grasp on reality had crumbled, or to that grasp's momentary return, River couldn't guess. After a lifetime hoarding secrets the old spook had lost himself among them, and no longer knew which truths he was concealing, which lies he was casting abroad. He and his late wife, Rose, had raised River, their only grandchild. Sitting with him in Skylarks' garden, a blanket covering the old man's knees, an iron curtain shrouding half his history, River felt adrift. He had followed the O.B.'s footsteps into the Secret Service, and if his own path had been forcibly rerouted, there'd been comfort in the knowledge that the old man had at least mapped the same territory. But now he was orphaned. The footsteps he'd followed were wandering in circles, and when they faltered at last, they'd be nowhere specific. Every spook's dream was to throw off all pursuers, and know himself unwatched. The O.B. was fast approaching that space: somewhere unknowable, unvisited, untagged by hostile eyes.

It had been a warm morning, bright sunshine casting shadows on the lawn. The house was at the end of a valley, and River could see hills rising in the distance, and tame clouds puffing across a paint box sky. A train was briefly visible between two stretches of woodland, but its engines were no more than a polite murmur, barely bothering the air. River could smell mown grass, and something else he couldn't put a name to. If forced to guess, he'd say it was the absence of traffic.

He sat on one of three white plastic chairs arranged around a white plastic table, from the centre of which a parasol jutted upwards. The third chair was vacant. There were two other similar sets of furniture, one unused, and the other occupied by an elderly couple. A younger woman was there, addressing them in what River imagined was an efficient tone. He couldn't actually hear her. His grandfather was talking loudly, blocking out all other conversation.

"That would have been August '52," he was saying. "The fifteenth, if I'm not mistaken. A Tuesday. Round about four o'clock in the afternoon."

The O.B.'s memory was self-sharpening these days. It prided itself on providing minute detail, even if that detail bore only coincidental resemblance to reality.

"And when the call came in, it was Joe himself on the line."

". . . Joe?"

"Stalin, my boy. You're not dropping off on me, are you?"

River wasn't dropping off on him.

He thought: this is where life on Spook Street leads. Not long ago the old man's past had come barking from the shadows and taken large bites out of the present. If this were common knowledge, there would be many howling for retribution. River should be among them, really. But if his own murky beginnings had turned out to be the result of the O.B.'s tampering with the lives of others, they remained his own beginnings. You couldn't argue yourself out of existence. Besides, there was no way of taking his grandfather to task for past sins now those sins had melted into fictions. The previous week, River had heard a story the old man had never told before, involving more gunfire than usual, and an elaborate series of code names in notebooks. Ten minutes on Google later revealed that the O.B. had been relaying the plot of *Where Eagles Dare*.

When the old man's tale wound itself into silence, River said, "Do you have everything you need, grandad?"

"Why should I need anything? Eh?"

"No reason. I just thought you might like something from . . ."

He tailed off. Something from home. But home was dangerous territory, a subject best avoided. The old man had never been a joe; always a desk man. It had been his job to send agents into the unknown, and run them from what others might think a safe distance. But here he was now, alone in joe country, his cover blown, his home untenable. There was no safe ground. Only this mansion house in a quiet landscape, where the nurses had enough discretion to know that some tales were best ignored.

On the train heading back into London, River shifted in his seat and scrolled down the page of search results. Nice to know that a spook career granted him this privilege: if he wanted to know what was going on, he could surf the web, like any other bastard. And the internet was screaming. The hunt for the Abbotsfield killers continued with no concrete results, though the attack had been claimed by so-called Islamic State. At a late-night session in Parliament the previous evening, Dennis Gimball had lambasted the Security Services, proclaiming Claude Whelan, Regent's Park's First Desk, unfit for purpose; had sailed this close to suggesting that he was, in fact, an IS sympathiser. That this was barking mad was a side issue: recent years had seen a recalibration of political lunacy, and even the mainstream media had to pretend to take Gimball seriously, just in case. Meanwhile, there were twelve dead in Abbotsfield, and a tiny village had become a geopolitical byword. There'd be a lot more debate, a lot more hand-wringing, before this slipped away from the front pages. Unless something else happened soon, of course.

Nearly there. River closed his laptop. The O.B. would be dozing again by now; enjoying a cat's afternoon in the sun. Time had rolled round on him, that was all. River was his grandfather's handler now.

Sooner or later, all the sins of the past fell into the keeping of the present.

"You stupid cow!"

He'd been thrown sideways and the noise in his head had exploded: manic guitars cut off midwail; locomotive drums killed midbeat. The sudden silence was deafening. It was like he'd been unplugged.

And his prey was nowhere to be seen, obviously. His smart-phone was in pieces, its casing a hop-skip-jump away.

It was Shirley Dander who'd leaped on him, evidently unable to control her passion.

She crawled off and pretended to be watching a car disappear along the road. Roddy sat up and brushed at the sleeves of his still-new leather jacket. He'd had to deal with workplace harassment before: first Louisa Guy, now this. But at least Louisa remained the right side of her last shaggable day, while Shirley Dander, far as the Rodster was concerned, hadn't seen her first yet.

"What the hell was that for?"

"That was me saving your arse," she said, without looking round.

His arse. One-track mind.

"I nearly had it, you know!" Pointless explaining the intricacies of a quest to her: the nearest she'd come to appreciating the complexities of gaming was being mistaken for a troll. Still, though, she ought to be made to realise just what a prize she'd cost him, all for the sake of a quick grope. "A bulbasaur! You know how rare that is?"

It was plain she didn't.

"The fuck," she asked, "are you talking about?"

He scrambled to his feet.

"Okay," he said. "Let's pretend you just wanted to sabotage my hunt. That's all Kim needs to know, anyway."

". . . Huh?"

"My girlfriend," he explained, so she'd know where she stood.

"Did you get a plate for that car?"

"What car?"

"The one that just tried to run you over."

"That's a good story too," Roddy said. "But let's stick with mine. It's less complicated. Fewer follow-up questions."

And having delivered this lesson in tradecraft, he collected the pieces of his phone and headed back to Slough House.

Where the day is well established now, and dawn a forgotten intruder. When River returns to take up post at his desk—his current task being so mind-crushingly dull, so balls-achingly unlikely to result in useful data, that he can barely remember what it is even while doing it—all the slow horses are back in the stable, and the hum of collective ennui is almost audible. Up in his attic room, Jackson Lamb scrapes the last sporkful of chicken fried rice from a foil dish, then tosses the container into a corner dark enough that it need never trouble his conscience again, should such a creature come calling, while two floors below Shirley Dander's face is scrunched into a thoughtful scowl as she replays in her mind the sequence of events that led to her flattening Roderick Ho: always a happy outcome, of course, but had she really prevented a car doing the same? Or had it just been another of London's penis-propelled drivers, whose every excursion onto the capital's roads morphs into a demolition derby? Maybe she should share the question with someone. Catherine Standish, she decides. Louisa Guy too, perhaps. Louisa might be an ironclad bitch at times, but at least she doesn't think with a dick. Some days, you take what you can.

Later, Lamb will host one of his occasional departmental meetings, its main purpose to ensure the ongoing discontent of all involved, but for now Slough House is what passes for peaceful, the grousing and grumbling of its denizens remaining mainly internal. The clocks that each of the crew separately watches dawdle through their paces on Slough House time, this being slower by some fifty percent than in most other places, while, like the O.B. in distant Berkshire, the day catnaps the afternoon away.

Elsewhere, mind, it's scurrying around like a demented gremlin.

Other Titles in the Soho Crime Series

Michael Genelin
(Slovakia)
Siren of the Waters
Dark Dreams
The Magician's Accomplice
Requiem for a Gypsy

Timothy Hallinan
(Thailand)
The Fear Artist
For the Dead
The Hot Countries
Fools' River

(Los Angeles)
Crashed
Little Elvises
The Fame Thief
Herbie's Game
King Maybe
Fields Where They Lay
Nighttown

Mette Ivie Harrison
(Mormon Utah)
The Bishop's Wife
His Right Hand
For Time and All Eternities
Not of This Fold

Mick Herron
(England)
Slow Horses
Dead Lions
Real Tigers
Spook Street
London Rules

Down Cemetery Road
The Last Voice You Hear
Why We Die
Smoke and Whispers

Reconstruction
Nobody Walks
This Is What Happened

Stan Jones
(Alaska)
White Sky, Black Ice
Shaman Pass
Frozen Sun

Stan Jones cont.
Village of the Ghost Bears
Tundra Kill
The Big Empty

**Lene Kaaberbøl &
Agnete Friis**
(Denmark)
The Boy in the Suitcase
Invisible Murder
Death of a Nightingale
The Considerate Killer

Martin Limón
(South Korea)
Jade Lady Burning
Slicky Boys
Buddha's Money
The Door to Bitterness
The Wandering Ghost
G.I. Bones
Mr. Kill
The Joy Brigade
Nightmare Range
The Iron Sickle
The Ville Rat
Ping-Pong Heart
The Nine-Tailed Fox
The Line

Ed Lin
(Taiwan)
Ghost Month
Incensed
99 Ways to Die

Peter Lovesey
(England)
The Circle
The Headhunters
False Inspector Dew
Rough Cider
On the Edge
The Reaper

(Bath, England)
The Last Detective
Diamond Solitaire
The Summons
Bloodhounds
Upon a Dark Night

Peter Lovesey cont.
The Vault
Diamond Dust
The House Sitter
The Secret Hangman
Skeleton Hill
Stagestruck
Cop to Corpse
The Tooth Tattoo
The Stone Wife
*Down Among
the Dead Men*
Another One Goes Tonight
Beau Death

(London, England)
Wobble to Death
*The Detective Wore
Silk Drawers*
Abracadaver
Mad Hatter's Holiday
The Tick of Death
A Case of Spirits
Swing, Swing Together
Waxwork

Jassy Mackenzie
(South Africa)
Random Violence
Stolen Lives
The Fallen
Pale Horses
Bad Seeds

Sujata Massey
(1920s Bombay)
*The Widows of
Malabar Hill*

Francine Mathews
(Nantucket)
Death in the Off-Season
Death in Rough Water
Death in a Mood Indigo
Death in a Cold Hard Light
Death on Nantucket

Seichō Matsumoto
(Japan)
*Inspector Imanishi
Investigates*

Magdalen Nabb
(Italy)
Death of an Englishman
Death of a Dutchman
Death in Springtime
Death in Autumn
*The Marshal and
the Murderer*
*The Marshal and
the Madwoman*
The Marshal's Own Case
*The Marshal Makes
His Report*
*The Marshal
at the Villa Torrini*
Property of Blood
Some Bitter Taste
The Innocent
Vita Nuova
The Monster of Florence

Fuminori Nakamura
(Japan)
The Thief
Evil and the Mask
Last Winter, We Parted
The Kingdom
The Boy in the Earth
Cult X

Stuart Neville
(Northern Ireland)
*The Ghosts of Belfast
Collusion
Stolen Souls
The Final Silence
Those We Left Behind
So Say the Fallen*

(Dublin)
Ratlines

Rebecca Pawel
(1930s Spain)
*Death of a Nationalist
Law of Return
The Watcher in the Pine
The Summer Snow*

Kwei Quartey
(Ghana)
*Murder at Cape
Three Points
Gold of Our Fathers
Death by His Grace*

Qiu Xiaolong
(China)
*Death of a Red Heroine
A Loyal Character Dancer
When Red Is Black*

John Straley
(Sitka, Alaska)
*The Woman Who Married
a Bear
The Curious Eat Themselves
The Music of What Happens
Death and the Language of
Happiness
The Angels Will Not Care
Cold Water Burning
Baby's First Felony*

(Cold Storage, Alaska)
*The Big Both Ways
Cold Storage, Alaska*

Akimitsu Takagi
(Japan)
*The Tattoo Murder Case
Honeymoon to Nowhere
The Informer*

Helene Tursten
(Sweden)
*Detective Inspector Huss
The Torso
The Glass Devil
Night Rounds
The Golden Calf
The Fire Dance
The Beige Man
The Treacherous Net
Who Watcheth
Protected by the Shadows*

Hunting Game

Helene Tursten cont.
*An Elderly Lady Is Up to
No Good*

**Janwillem van de
Wetering**
(Holland)
*Outsider in Amsterdam
Tumbleweed
The Corpse on the Dike
Death of a Hawker
The Japanese Corpse
The Blond Baboon
The Maine Massacre
The Mind-Murders
The Streetbird
The Rattle-Rat
Hard Rain
Just a Corpse at Twilight
Hollow-Eyed Angel
The Perfidious Parrot
The Sergeant's Cat:
Collected Stories*

Timothy Williams
(Guadeloupe)
*Another Sun
The Honest Folk
of Guadeloupe*

(Italy)
*Converging Parallels
The Puppeteer
Persona Non Grata
Black August
Big Italy
The Second Day
of the Renaissance*

Jacqueline Winspear
(1920s England)
*Maisie Dobbs
Birds of a Feather*